TOWN TAMER

by

Jack Holt

Dales Large Print Books
Long Preston, North Yorkshire,
BD23 4ND, England.

British Library Cataloguing in Publication Data.

Holt, Jack
    Town tamer.

    A catalogue record of this book is
    available from the British Library

    ISBN   978-1-84262-536-1 pbk

First published in Great Britain in 2005 by Robert Hale Limited

Copyright © James O'Brien 2005

Cover illustration © Gordon Crabb by arrangement with
Alison Eldred

Published in Large Print 2007 by arrangement with
Robert Hale Ltd.

Dales Large Print is an imprint of Library Magna Books Ltd.

Printed and bound in Great Britain by
T.J. (International) Ltd., Cornwall, PL28 8RW

PROLOGUE

Marshal Sam Brody ended his report to the Town Council on a sombre note:

'The fact is that Lance Roebuck and his hard-cases are a problem, and getting to be a bigger problem with each passing day. And I reckon that turning a blind eye to Roebuck's shenanigans is a policy that this town will come to regret one day soon.'

The meeting had been two years earlier.

'Talk to old Nathan Roebuck, Sam,' Ned Drucker the council chairman urged the marshal for what must have been the hundredth time in as many meetings over recent months. 'Get him to rein in his nephew.'

Brody shook his head, his patience short.

'I've already done that more than once, Ned. It's not that Nathan Roebuck ain't willing to rein in Lance. It's that he can't.

Lance Roebuck's out of order and out of line, and Nathan ain't a young man anymore.'

'If Lance is that much of a nuisance, why doesn't the old man kick him off his range?' Willie Sneed the owner of the town livery wondered. 'And if that doesn't work, then whip him 'til his back is raw.'

Sam Brody opined: 'There was a time when Nathan Roebuck would have done that, Willie. But he's an old man now, needing company. And when a man gets to that stage, it's hard for him to see any wrong in the last kin he's got.

'Maybe, he's fearful of Lance Roebuck's revenge too, should any attempt by him to rein his nephew in backfire.'

'Something must be done,' Sneed pressed.

Brody's eyes swept the meeting.

'You're the Town Council. You fellas decide, and I'll do the doing.'

'And what would *you* recommend, Sam?'

The question came from Nils Pederson, the town blacksmith.

'No disrespect intended, Nils,' Brody grunted. 'But you gents haven't listened to what I had to say in the past, and I just plumb got fed up of saying it.'

Pederson said: 'But bringing Roebuck to book, Sam, would not be easy. He can call on at least fifty men. Twenty of whom are gun-handy.'

'Dealing with a viper like Lance Roebuck will never be easy,' said Brody. 'That's why, if we do decide to deal with him, every man has to be of one mind.'

Shifting backsides were the order. Sam Brody was witnessing nothing new, he'd been a lawman in four towns in his career as a badge-toter, and towns ran pretty much true to form. Everyone wanted something done, but no one was willing to lend a hand to do it. They put a badge on a man, and figured that he should throw away his life for the miserly wage they paid. Well, Brody thought, good law and a safe town is every man's responsibility. Besides, being abso-lutely honest with himself, he wasn't at all sure that he could tame Lance Roebuck. Maybe if the council had acted a couple of years earlier, when he had predicted the path that Roebuck would take, that gent would never have turned bad to begin with. Back then the members of the Town Council had accused their marshal of being alarmist. But the fact was that Sam Brody had seen many Lance Roebucks in his time. And he had also seen the same mistake made as many times, too.

It was Ned Drucker, who was now avoiding his gaze, who had said back then: 'Oh, Sam. It's just Lance having some high jinks.'

He had answered angrily: 'Beating a man to within an inch of his life because he bumped against him and spilled his drink is a lot more than high jinks!'

'I think it would be unwise to get too heavy-handed, Marshal,' the council chairman had said. 'After all, the man in question was just a no-good drifter. And Lance Roebuck, in the not-too-distant future, will be the boss of the biggest spread in this territory.'

Meaning that business from the Roebuck ranch would fill the coffers of the businessmen who made up the Town Council.

Drucker had added, darkly, 'As marshal, Sam, I reckon you should take your guidance from this council.'

Sam Brody recalled how the urge to buck the council or hand back his badge was overpowering. But to his shame he had thought of his age and pension, and had dodged doing the right thing. So that made him as guilty as everyone else.

Drucker had become lavish in his praise.

'You're the best lawman that this town has ever had, Sam. And we're darn lucky to have a marshal with your kind of sterling qualities to make for peaceful nights in our beds.' His views had received the council's unstinting endorsement. 'In fact,' Drucker went on, 'I figure that a ten-dollar raise is in order.'

'If we could only get Lucy Bracken into Lance Roebuck's arms our problems would be solved,' Charles P. Taylor, the town banker now sighed.

Nodding heads vouched for the wisdom of Taylor's view.

Willie Sneed said: 'There's no way that that's going to happen. That gal's heart belongs only to Dan Clancy. Must be touched in the head, I'd say,' he concluded. 'Hankering after the town drunk.'

Now as he walked towards the saloon where the latest bout of Roebuck maliciousness was being acted out, Sam Brody bitterly regretted having not stood up to the Town Council. Because since that time, Lance Roebuck had slid further and further down the slippery pole of devilry. The town was becoming a magnet for other hardcases, too, some had come at Roebuck's invitation, others had become aware of townfolk too afraid or too enriched by Roebuck largess to act, and a marshal who was hog-tied by the Town Council and nearing the end of his days as a lawman. All in all Watts Bend was becoming a wide open town; a town where good times were to be had, and a man did not have to worry too much about retribution when he enjoyed the protection of one of its most prominent citizens, who just happened to be rotten to the core.

Brody was on his way to help a man who, a long time ago now, he had thought of having as his deputy.

'A saddle-tramp with a badge!' had been the awed response, when he had proposed Dan Clancy's nomination as his deputy.

'Clancy ain't a saddle-tramp,' he'd argued. 'He's a man looking to put down roots.'

'Clancy's a saddle-tramper,' Ned Drucker had repeated, doggedly.

'I think he's a good man who's fallen on hard times,' Brody had opined. 'There's a difference. Besides, he's fast with a gun.'

'Now where would he have learned gun-craft like his?' Nils Pederson had questioned.

'Prob'ly as a hired killer,' Ben Atkins, the council's most senior member and a founding father of the town, snorted.

A lot of water had flowed under the bridge since that turning-point meeting, most of it bad. And all of it bad for Dan Clancy.

CHAPTER ONE

Dan Clancy licked lips as parched as desert sand. His eyes followed the intentional dribble of whiskey, which Lance Roebuck had let trickle down his chin. Clancy cursed the waste. The trickle formed a golden drop on the point of Roebuck's chin and Clancy fought the urge to lick it off. His whiskey-craving innards quaked – his thirst was a needle going deep into his brain. His throat constricted to cut off his breath and his eyes were filled with the vacant, anguished pleading of the addicted.

Roebuck looked at Clancy the way a man would look at manure on his boot. There was no mercy or kindness in the cold grey eyes, only mocking. He spilled his drink over Dan Clancy's head and Clancy's tongue shamelessly snatched at every drop rolling down his face, he then used his hands to try and channel any stray drops of the whiskey into his mouth.

'You know, fellas,' Lance Roebuck said to his coterie of hardcases, 'I figure that if I poured that whiskey down my pants, I'd have me the cleanest ass in the territory.'

Wild laughter erupted and spread throughout the saloon with the rapidity of a bushfire in a drought.

'Other places you could've poured it too,' the sniggering sidekick, who had alerted Roebuck to Dan Clancy's yearning, said. 'Mebbe save ya the dollars you'll be payin' the blonde dove you've been eyein' all night, Lance.'

Frank Dawson's lurid scenario raised another bout of even wilder laughter.

'Well, now, Frank,' Roebuck chuckled. 'Why do you think I'm going to Lily's room with a bottle of whiskey?'

By now the saloon was rocking with laughter. But Lance Roebuck, a mean-minded, cruel bastard of a man saw yet another opportunity for jocularity at Dan Clancy's expense. He signalled to the barkeep for a bottle, which he held up in front of Clancy, waving it mesmerically back and forth across the drunk's eyes.

'It's all yours, Clancy,' Roebuck tempted. 'All you've got to do is–' He thought about what he wanted the drunk to do which would be most degrading. Then, he said: 'I've got it. Lily,' he called to the dove with whom he intended to dally, 'fetch one of those fancy frilly dresses you've got.'

'Why, Lance?'

'Heck, Lily, didn't you hear. Clancy here is going to sing for his supper.' He uncorked the bottle and drew it across Dan Clancy's nostrils. 'Ain't that so, Clancy?'

There was an ocean of shame in Dan Clancy's eyes. But his need for the liquor over-rode his pride and every other need in him.

'Sure, Lance,' he croaked. 'Sure, I'll sing.'

'In Lily's dress,' Roebuck stressed.

Clancy hesitated. Roebuck dipped his

finger in the bottle and then placed it on Clancy's lips.

'Yeah, yeah. Sure,' the drunk eagerly agreed.

'Go get that dress, Lily,' Roebuck urged. 'And bring along that box of tricks you make yourself pretty with.' He sniggered. 'I want Clancy to look real purty when he sings.'

The Roebuck hardcases were holding on to the bar, they were so overcome with laughter. Some of the other imbibers went along with Lance Roebuck's cruel antics, but there were some men who were uneasy with his shenanagins who did not have the courage to speak out – bucking Lance Roebuck had proven unhealthy.

However, there was one man stepping through the batwings, who was not afraid to tangle with Roebuck. He had done it a couple of times before. Some said that it was a loco thing for Marshal Sam Brody to do, and many of the marshal's friends had warned him against doing it again.

'No need for Dan to sing for his supper,'

Brody said. 'I've heard him sing, and I've had prisoners breaking wind who sounded more musical.'

Lance Roebuck glared at Brody, an evil fire in his eyes.

'A deal's been struck, Marshal,' he said.

'A deal isn't a deal until a man shakes hands on it, Roebuck,' Brody declared. He turned to Dan Clancy. 'Dan, I've got a whole pile of chores that I haven't the time now or never will have to get round to doing: like a backyard that needs tending; and slates that need fixing; trees and bushes that need trimming; and a house that needs painting. And I reckon that you're the man I'm looking for to do these chores, Dan.'

He beckoned to the barkeep for a bottle and handed it to Clancy.

'Down-payment,' Sam Brody said. 'How does seven o'clock tomorrow morning sound, Dan?'

Clancy, hugging the bottle, nodded his head in agreement and Brody held out his hand to shake. Clancy shook it. 'Seven o'clock, Sam.'

'That's a deal, Dan.'

'I'm not sure I like you stepping on my tail, Marshal,' Lance Roebuck said with quiet menace.

Brody stated bluntly: 'I don't much care what you like or dislike, Roebuck.' He told Dan Clancy: 'When I say seven o'clock, I mean seven o'clock, Dan.'

'Seven o'clock it'll be, Marshal Brody,' Clancy promised.

'I might still be in the blankets,' Brody said. 'But don't let that stop you beginning work. I'll leave the kitchen door open. You make yourself some breakfast, Dan. A man needs a full belly if he's to work the way I'll make you work. Ten dollars work for every dollar paid.'

Dan Clancy wiped away a tear from his cheek.

'You'll get twenty dollars work for every dollar, Marshal. That I promise you.'

Brody nodded. 'I know I will, Dan. I know I will.' The marshal turned and marched out of the saloon. No sooner had he left than Lance Roebuck, bristling and spiteful, grabbed the bottle of whiskey from Clancy and smashed it on the bartop. Goaded, the drunk went for Roebuck's throat. But weakened by rough living, poor diet and too much liquor, Roebuck had no difficulty in brushing Clancy aside. He caught Clancy in an armlock and pitched him across the saloon upending several tables, spilling the drinks on them. Still no one dared object to Roebuck's loutish behaviour.

'Kick him out,' Roebuck ordered two of his cronies.

Two burly cow-punchers stepped forward and ran Clancy out of the saloon with enough momentum to propel him into the middle of Main Street where he crashed heavily to the ground.

Dan Clancy lay curled up on the street, unable to stand up until the fire inside his gut had eased. A stray, mangy dog came to sniff at him and cocked his leg. Clancy felt the hot flush of the animal's urine on his face. He curled up more, shame now added to his thirst.

'Dan...'

Clancy felt Lucy Bracken's soft touch, but did not open his eyes to look at her. Right now he had more than enough hurt and shame to deal with.

'Go away, Lucy,' he said, making himself sound as grumpy and as unsociable as he could. 'You shouldn't be out in the street. Go back to that nice feather bed of yours. You're decent folk, Lucy.'

'I'll brew up some coffee if you come inside, Dan.'

'You wouldn't want the smell of me round that pretty house of yours.'

'Well, I've got soap and water if you're of a mind to get round that problem,' Lucy Bracken said, sharp tongued and annoyed by Clancy's refusal of help.

Dan Clancy laughed a sad laugh.

'Ain't much point in wasting soap and water on me, Lucy,' he said. 'I'll be every bit as filthy after my next binge.'

The dog came back and Lucy angrily shooed him away. She stooped to help Clancy up.

'Leave me be!' he snarled, shrugging her off.

'Maybe I will at that,' Lucy said, tears catching her voice. 'Seems you're hellbound anyway, Dan Clancy. And you're not going to let anyone stop you!'

Clancy looked after Lucy as she stormed back to her dressmaker's shop, and a mountain of memories flooded into his mind.

It was a windy late fall day.

'Ma, pa's duds are dry.'

Dan Clancy's memory of that day, riding past the Bracken house on his way into Watts Bend, swept back. And he saw again with sparkling clarity, the breathtaking vision of Lucy Bracken. His whiskey-befuddled brain could not remember much anymore, but the sight of Lucy had been burned into it. And Clancy figured that when his time came to meet his Maker, the sight of Lucy Bracken on that day would be his last thought on earth.

'Want me to bring them in, Ma?' the red-haired girl enquired of the matronly woman standing in the open door of the house, whose hair, though grey now, still showed hints of the flame it once had; just like the younger woman's, Clancy reckoned.

'Not from that mud you dropped your father's trousers in,' said the matronly, florid-faced woman.

Flustered, Lucy bent to retrieve the mud-died trousers. And Clancy recalled now how pleased it had made him that the red-haired woman had had her concentration on the task in hand scattered as he rode past.

'Howdy, stranger,' the older woman called out. 'Storm building, I figure.'

'Seems so, ma'am,' Dan Clancy had replied sociably.

'Where are you from?' she enquired.

'Montana, ma'am.'

'You're a long way from home.'

Dan crouched in the saddle and shivered as

a sudden gust of wind sprinkled rain on him.

'You'd better drop by Ned Drucker's store and get yourself some longjohns,' the woman said. 'Nothing like Drucker's drawers to keep out the wind.'

'Ma!' Lucy had yelled, shocked at her ma's boldness.

'Oh shoo, girl,' Martha Bracken scolded her daughter. 'Ain't no shame to be in them. Sure is, if you're out of them though, and ain't supposed to be.'

She laughed with gusto. Lucy fled the yard, trailing her father's clothes behind her in her hurry.

'Darn, Lucy,' her ma wailed. 'You'd best wash your pa's duds again. Like to step inside for some fresh apple pie, Mr...?'

'Clancy, ma'am. Dan Clancy. And I'd be surely obliged for a slice of apple pie.'

'Martha Bracken,' the woman informed him, as he got down from his horse. 'And that's my daughter Lucy getting all flustered.'

Clancy tipped his hat to Lucy, who had ventured back into the yard.

'Ma'am.'

'Ma'am!' Lucy yelped. 'I ain't that old, mister.'

'Miss, then.'

'That's better.'

'Watch your manners young lady,' Martha Bracken rebuked her daughter. 'Mr Clancy is our guest.'

Martha Bracken led the way into the kitchen. Immediately on entering, Dan Clancy was taken by its homely and welcoming atmosphere. He came up short on seeing the man sitting at the kitchen table.

'Lance Roebuck. Dan Clancy,' Martha introduced.

Dan had accepted Lance Roebuck's firm handshake.

'Pleased to meet you, Mr Roebuck,' Dan said.

'That'll be plain Lance, Mr Clancy,' Lance Roebuck had insisted.

'Then, that'll be plain Dan too, Lance.'

On that fall day, three years previously, there was not the merest hint of the acrimonious and trouble-strewn passage that was ahead for Dan Clancy. In fact on the evidence of that day, there was no way that either man could have foreseen the sour direction their lives would take.

Lucy entered the kitchen.

'Hi, Lucy,' Lance greeted her robustly. 'You look prettier than a summer rose.'

Lucy, just over one bout of fluster, was pitched right into another by Lance Roebuck's fawning compliment.

'It's not natural for a man to be so honey-tongued, Lance,' she rebuked Roebuck.

Unfazed, Roebuck replied, 'Every word's true, Lucy.'

Lucy's green eyes clashed with Clancy's.

'I'm sure that you wouldn't talk such nonsense, Mr Clancy?' she said.

'Nonsense?' Dan chuckled. 'Hardly. Lance got it exactly right, I reckon.'

'See?' Roebuck chanted triumphantly.

'Well... Well...' Lucy flung her hands in the air.

'Yes, Miss Bracken,' Clancy teased. 'You

were about to say.'

'Well... Oh, fiddly!'

'Does she always keep storming off like that, ma'am?' Clancy asked Martha Bracken, pitching his voice so that the departing Lucy could hear him.

'It's her way,' Martha sighed. 'Always has been. Got it from her Uncle Joe.' She grinned. 'We used to call him the door-slammer, seeing that he always seemed to be storming off somewhere, slamming doors.'

'Heck,' Lance Roebuck sighed. 'Ain't she awful pretty when she's riled.'

Now, pushing the memories from his mind because their pain was so awful, Dan Clancy got unsteadily to his feet. He was not drunk, but nowadays the lack of alcohol had the same dizzying effect on his brain.

Lance Roebuck had come on to the saloon porch in the company of his hardcases and hangers-on. He began to ape Clancy's shaky progress to an alley where he slept most nights, sharing it with dogs and rodents.

'You know what,' Roebuck said, 'I think

the streets in this town are getting more and more full of vermin.'

Lucy Bracken, who had not gone inside but had sought the shelter of her shop doorway, ached inside for Dan Clancy. And fumed at Lance Roebuck's cruel mockery.

'Don't forget, Clancy,' Roebuck called to him. 'You've got to be at the marshal's house by seven a.m. to earn that bottle of rotgut.'

'Heck, Lance,' a string of a man whose nature was polecat mean, sniggered. 'He ain't goin' to be on time the way he's movin'.'

'And I guess if he gets there,' said another of Roebuck's cronies, 'and tries to drive a nail, Brody will think he's got woodpeckers. But it'll only be Clancy missing that darn nail time and time again.'

Dan Clancy wobbled into the alley, his ears full of Roebuck's mocking laughter. When Dan was out of sight, Lucy Bracken stepped from the shadows to rebuke Roebuck.

'Haven't you got an iota of decency in you, Lance Roebuck,' she blasted him. 'You just pray that some day you won't have to suffer what Dan Clancy has to suffer. Because,' she said pointedly, 'you wouldn't be man enough to bear up under the burden!'

'Now listen here, Lucy,' Roebuck protested.

'Listen? I'd prefer to lie down with a snake instead of hearing anything you have to say,' Lucy railed. She slammed the shop door shut.

'What is it with that woman and slamming doors,' Roebuck grumbled.

A short while later, Lucy re-emerged carrying a bundle. She quickly made her way to the alley into which Clancy had staggered. Halfway along the alley she found him, curled up and shivering. She put the blanket she had brought with her over him. Tears welled up in her green eyes at the pitiful sight of the man she had fallen in love with that day he had accepted her ma's invitation to partake of apple pie.

The man who had broken her heart from that first moment he had entered her life.

CHAPTER TWO

'Staying 'round long, Dan?'

Her ma's enquiry had stilled Lucy Bracken's heartbeat, because she had been trying to ask the same question since she had set eyes on the stranger.

'Ain't sure yet, ma'am,' he'd replied. 'Ain't got a plan you could talk about.'

Lucy's fearful glance had gone to her ma, knowing how poorly she thought of drifters.

''Fraid of hard work,' was the opinion Lucy had often heard Martha Bracken express about men she considered to be drifters. And she would add contemptuously: 'Drifters!' And spit.

'Footloose, are ya?' Martha Bracken asked Dan Clancy, in the kind of casually disinterested tone she used when fishing for vital information.

31

Clancy had considered the term *footloose* for a spell, before answering: 'I'd say a man looking to put down roots, ma'am, would best describe me.'

It was Martha Bracken's turn to consider terms.

'You'd say, would you?'

'Yes, ma'am.'

She shoved a second helping of apple pie Clancy's way.

'Been looking long?' she enquired.

'A goodly spell,' Clancy answered.

Lucy noted the slight hesitation in the offering of apple pie, and feared that her ma would pull it back. When she did not, Lucy's relief was palpable.

'Ain't you got chores?' her ma asked Lucy.

'Most of them are done, Ma,' Lucy answered spiritedly, afraid that if she scurried away like she did when under her ma's steely glare, Dan Clancy would think her browbeaten. And she could in no way imagine that he would have anything to do with a woman whom he considered hadn't the grit to stand up for herself.

'Most of them ain't good enough, girl!' Martha Bracken said, her tone closer to berating than opining. 'Best get to them.'

Lucy now recalled Dan Clancy's maddeningly wry grin.

'Git, girl!' her ma ordered.

'Maybe I could lend a hand in return for this delicious apple pie,' Clancy had suggested.

'You'll want to be getting to town,' Martha Bracken said, when Dan got up to accompany Lucy.

The momentary leap of Lucy's heart was stilled by her ma's virtual dismissal of Dan Clancy from the house. It was obvious to Lucy that her ma had made up her mind that Dan was nothing better than the countless lazy no-goods who passed through Watts Bend, looking everywhich way to avoid letting their eyes be offended by work.

'Lance, you'll stay a spell,' Martha said, unambiguously stating her preference as to whom she reckoned was suitable company for her daughter. 'You'll help Lucy hoe the vegetable patch.'

Roebuck, accurately reading the situation, was cock-of-the-hoop.

'Thank you ma'am for your hospitality,' he said politely. 'Appreciate it.'

Clancy stood up to leave.

Lucy had shot her ma a pleading glance, and had got an icy glare in return. Defiantly, she said: 'The vegetable patch will have to wait, Ma. I've got some chores to do in town. That new cotton's come in to Drucker's store. And I need a new dress.'

She turned to Lance Roebuck.

'Of course you could always get a head start on the patch, Lance, if you've a mind to.'

Lance Roebuck's cocky grin faded, he grabbed his hat from the table and strode out of the kitchen. Martha Bracken was furious. Lucy had almost lost her nerve.

'You don't mind if I ride to town with you, Dan?'

Clancy, caught in a position he would not

have wished for, and seeing that he had high hopes of finding work and settling in town or maybe in a ranch in its hinterland, said:

'Oh, there'll always be cotton, Lucy. And the weeds will be much bigger and ten times tougher tomorrow.'

Stung, Lucy chanted, 'Is that a fact, Mr Clancy. Then I won't bother you any. I'll make my own way to town.'

Lucy recalled having stormed out of the kitchen, letting the door frame shudder. Martha Bracken said:

'It's for the best, Mr Clancy.'

Dan Clancy was not so sure that it was, as Martha Bracken said, for the best. He had not been sparked by a woman for a long time in such a spritely fashion as Lucy Bracken had sparked him. Maybe if he got a job and showed himself to be responsible and upstanding, Martha Bracken might find him more acceptable than the dog under the table, but he doubted it. She impressed him as being a woman who, once she made up her mind, seldom ever changed it.

'I guess,' he said, with little conviction.

Martha Bracken, picking up on Clancy's less than enthusiastic endorsement of her view, spoke bluntly:

'Mr Clancy, I expect that any attention Lucy will pay you, you'll reject out of hand,' she stated. 'And that you'll not follow any leanings you might have towards turning her head more than it's already been turned.

'Do I have your word, sir?'

Clancy nodded. 'You have my word, ma'am.'

'Then why don't you have another slice of apple pie.'

Clancy grinned ruefully.

'Don't think I will, ma'am.'

'Well, good day then,' Martha Bracken said, and turned away.

Dan Clancy left and was almost run down by Lucy charging out of the yard on a midnight black stallion. Clancy mounted up and left the yard at a more sedate pace, feeling the burn of Martha Bracken's eyes on his back, and the equally hot glare of

Lance Roebuck off to the side of the house rubbing his face where Clancy reckoned Lucy Bracken had slapped it.

Looking back now, Lucy knew that on that day, the bad blood between Lance Roebuck and Dan Clancy had begun to simmer and would eventually reach boiling point. To her discredit, she had done a whole lot to keep the pot of hatred bubbling, for a time playing one man off against the other.

'Still nursing lame dogs, Lucy?'

Lucy Bracken swung around to face a sneering Lance Roebuck.

'What I choose to do with my time is my business, Lance Roebuck,' Lucy trumpeted, and swept past him on her way out of the alley.

'Clancy would be better off dead, I reckon,' he said.

Lucy swung around, her green eyes blazing.

'You be his executioner,' she stated. 'And I'll be yours, Lance!'

A couple of Roebuck's cronies hiding in the shadows sniggered.

'Isn't it about time you and the trash you surround yourself with were crawling back into whatever hole you crawled out of,' Lucy railed.

One of the sniggering hardcases leapt from hiding, snarling and ready to do Lucy an injury. Roebuck's fist shot out to stagger him back against the wall of the general store.

'Thank you, Lance,' Lucy said. 'And I'll ask for your word that when I leave, you or your henchmen will not lay into Dan. Do I have your word?'

Roebuck nodded.

When they left the alley, Dan Clancy poked his head out from under the blanket. 'You're all kinds of a fool, Dan Clancy,' he murmured. 'You should have grabbed hold of that fine and good woman when you had the chance, and be damned to everyone who stood in your way!'

CHAPTER THREE

The night, for Dan Clancy, was one of terror. His craving for liquor sent shudder after shudder through him, until he was unable to unwind from the gut-clutching ball he had wound himself into. Demons welled up out of the darkness to assail him. First light, even though grey, was too much for him to open his eyes against. But burned deep into his brain was the promise he had made to Sam Brody. Promises made over the last couple of years had in the main been promises broken, as his every waking minute became consumed by his need for liquor. Until now the mangiest dog in town was more welcome inside than he was. Folk did not understand that his fever for liquor was more fierce than the most rabid fever that could afflict a man. But he could not blame anyone but himself for becoming the outcast he had turned out to be. There had been a time or two in his early days of slugging, when he had looked in the mirror and been ashamed of the man looking back at him; maybe he could have stopped his thirst in its tracks then, but he had been fool enough to think that there was no hurry, that he could end his love affair with liquor any time of his choosing. *No fool like an old fool* his pa had once told him, when he had over-mortgaged the ranch and lost it to the bank. And he had surely been right in that.

Slowly, Dan Clancy opened one eye and grimaced at the pain that shot through it, setting off clanging bells inside his skull. He was minded to shut it again and lay where he was until the town cleaner rousted him in an hour or so, but he fought against every instinct to linger.

'You've made Sam Brody a promise,' he growled in self-rebuke. 'And you're damn well going to keep that promise.'

Brody, a tough-as-nails lawman who gave

no ground to trouble-stirrers, was also the kindest of men to lame dogs. Many nights he had had Dan as his guest when a cell was available, and had thrown in breakfast at his own expense. He could have put it on the town slate, but Brody was an honest man who expected other men to be honest with him in return.

Sam Brody was the main reason that the people of Watts Bend lived their lives in peace and calm. Brody and Roebuck had locked horns a couple of times, but the viperish rancher had had the good sense to not push all the way. However, one day he might, and it was that possibility – especially of late as Roebuck got more and more stroppish – that occupied many hours of talk in the homes, stores and saloon. It had almost got to that point the previous night when Brody had stepped in to end his humiliation at the hands of Lance Roebuck. There was that split-second in which he had seen the glint of possibility in Roebuck's eyes as his brain calculated his chances of out-drawing Brody, whose draw, though having slowed some in recent times, was still one of the fastest in the territory. A lot of plots in the town's cemetery were filled with men who thought they had had the measure of Sam Brody, to discover to their cost that all they really had had was a pipe dream.

As he got to his feet, crouched over, Dan Clancy's groan came from the very pit of his stomach. Slowly and agonizingly he cranked his spine straight, except for the curve at the very top of his back that was the result of being huddled up with a bottle or scrounging dregs on a bartop for too long. Maybe, too, from raiding the town café trash-cans for scraps.

On legs as wobbly as an old, old-timer, Clancy made his way along the alley to its meeting with Main Street, where the full blast of the rising sun sent him scurrying back into the shadowed alley from where he crept forward, meeting the sun an inch at the time.

Seated at her bedroom window, where she

had sat huddled in a blanket fearing Lance Roebuck would go back on his word, Lucy Bracken watched with a pain-filled heart Dan Clancy's staggering progress along Main Street towards the marshal's house at its south end.

'Oh, Dan, my darling,' she wept.

A time or two, when he looked like toppling over, Lucy was out of her chair and ready to race to his assistance. But he kept going on his erratic way until he reached Sam Brody's house. Only then did her apprehension ease: Brody was a fine man and an equally fine Christian, he would look after Dan. There was a time when Brody had wanted Dan as his deputy, but the Town Council had rejected the idea.

Lucy's attention turned to Lance Roebuck leaving the saloon, a dove on his arm to kiss him goodbye. Spotting Lucy at the window, his kiss became passionate and prolonged. Lucy feigned indifference. But in her heart she was hurting too for Lance Roebuck. Because in his way, though his was not as dramatic a fall from grace as Dan Clancy's, he too was only a shadow of the man he might have been had Dan not passed by the house that fateful day three years ago. Had he chosen another route into town she would probably now be Mrs Lance Roebuck, instead of longing to be Mrs Dan Clancy. Not that she regretted not being Lance Roebuck's wife. But she did regret, and bitterly so, the rotten twist of fate that had robbed her of the chance to be Dan's wife.

'Sam,' Clancy called out, finding the eerie silence of the marshal's house unsettling. 'Are you up and respectable?' he called upstairs.

Clancy was hesitant to go upstairs because Sam Brody was a man who liked his privacy. Sometimes, though Sam thought it was a secret, Molly Barnes, a widow woman, visited late at night when the town was fast asleep, and the next morning pretended that she had come to clean for Sam as a means to leave the house with her respectability and Sam Brody's reputation intact. Sam would come to the door as she was leaving and holler:

'You sure got every speck of dust, Molly?'

Her reply was always the same.

'Every darn speck, Marshal.'

It was a scene which amused the townfolk. But the citizens' respect for both Sam and Molly kept tongues from wagging. It had amazed most people that Lance Roebuck or one of his hardcases had not slung dirt at Brody to embarrass him. But the common wisdom was that Roebuck and his cronies feared the towering rage which any snideness would likely raise in the marshal. Time had taught that it was a fool who purposefully irked Sam Brody.

'Sam,' Dan Clancy called again, 'are you up there?'

His summons getting no response, Clancy went upstairs one careful step at a time, ready to sprint back downstairs should he be an unwelcome intruder. On reaching midpoint on the stairs and being eye level with the landing, he could see that the door of Sam's bedroom was ajar. And that was something the marshal never did, sleep with an open room door. In essence he was a very private man, and in Clancy's previous visits he had observed the lawman's rituals of privacy to the letter.

'Sam,' he called in a whisper. 'Are you awake?'

Still no response. So Clancy continued on to the landing outside the bedroom. It was then that his nostrils flared at the scent of blood. He eased open the door and gagged: Sam Brody was lying across the blood-drenched bed, a wide, ugly gash on his throat. The blood had congealed and had formed thick black lumps of gore on the awful wound. The blood had also dried on the sheets. This told Clancy that Sam Brody's murder had taken place some hours previously. The window was firmly shut, so the blood had dried without the aid of a draught. It was late summer, edging into fall. The night had been cool, so there had been no heat either to dry the blood. How long did blood take to dry? he wondered. An hour? Two? Maybe three? There was a lot of blood. Judging by the marshal's stark pallor, every drop of his blood had been spilled.

'Marshal!'

Dan Clancy froze on hearing Lance Roebuck call out.

'Marshal. It's Lance Roebuck. I've come to make my apologies before leaving town. Don't want no bad blood between us now.'

Footsteps on the stairs.

A voice shouting inside Clancy's head was telling him to get out. He was a drunk, a man of no standing, in a room with a dead body. And he was about to be discovered by the nephew of the territory's richest cattle baron. Clancy hurried to the window and raised it as quietly as he could with only seconds remaining for him to make his escape.

'Marshal, are you still in the hay?'

The room door was opening when Dan Clancy vanished through the window, dropping straight to the ground. The long drop jarred every bone in his body and he felt his right ankle turn under the pressure. He hobbled away and rounding the corner of the house, ran straight into Jack Stone, Lance Roebuck's chief trouble-stirrer, who was leaning against the gable end puffing on a Mexican cheroot.

'Why, howdy, Clancy,' Stone greeted affably. 'You seem to be in a heck of a hurry.'

Just then Lance Roebuck leaned out the bedroom window.

'Murder,' he hollered. 'Murder's been done!'

Instantly, Jack Stone's sixgun flashed in his hand and was levelled on Dan Clancy. 'Twitch and I'll blast you, Clancy,' he growled. He shoved Dan ahead of him, the barrel of the .45 poking his spine. 'I've got your stinkin' murderer, Lance. He was lightin' out right now.'

'That a fact,' Roebuck gloated. 'You keep that gun on him, Jack.'

Roebuck vanished from the window and

appeared in the back yard seconds later, just when folk who had been alerted by his holler were arriving to verify the veracity of his claim.

'Sam Brody is upstairs,' he told the first arrivals. 'But I warn you, it ain't a pretty sight to behold.'

'Did Clancy kill Sam?' a man asked Roebuck.

'I figure he did,' was Lance Roebuck's reply. 'He must have been right in the marshal's bedroom while I was on my way upstairs. He fled through the bedroom window. Just as well that Jack Stone was on hand to witness his sneaky flight from the scene of his crime.'

'I didn't kill Sam,' Dan Clancy asserted. 'He was already dead for hours when I got here.'

Roebuck scoffed. 'Tall tales ain't going to help you now, Clancy.'

'Why would Clancy want to murder the marshal, Mr Roebuck?' a second man wondered. 'Sam was about the only man in town who had any time for him.'

'Probably to rob him,' Roebuck suggested. 'I've seen drunks willing to do anything to get their hands on a bottle.'

There was a nodding, of heads in agreement.

'Dan...'

Clancy swung around at the sound of Lucy Bracken's voice. Stone clipped him on the side of the head with the barrel of his pistol. Clancy staggered backwards. Lucy steadied him.

'There was no call for that, Stone,' she berated Lance Roebuck's henchman.

'Can't take a chance with a murderer, Lucy,' a woman in the ever-growing crowd said. 'That drunk is a desperate man.'

Shocked, Lucy intoned: 'Murderer?' She turned to Dan Clancy for an explanation.

'It's not true, Lucy,' he assured her.

Lance Roebuck again stated the sequence of events, and Dan saw the doubt creep into Lucy's eyes.

'There's no doubting but that he mur-

dered the marshal, Lucy,' Roebuck concluded.

Lucy was shaking her head in disbelief.

'It ain't so, Lucy,' Clancy again assured
her.

'Jack,' Roebuck said, 'would you be willing
to act as marshal until an election can take
place to find ourselves a new badge-toter?'

'I'd see it as my duty to pin on a star to see
this killer get his just dues, Lance.'

'Good. That's settled. So you'd best lock
up your prisoner, Marshal Stone,' Roebuck
declared. 'We wouldn't want a man of his
dangerous kind busting loose and running
round town to murder more good folk.'

'Move!' Jack Stone ordered Dan Clancy.

'Judge Fleming over in Kiowa Falls should
only take a couple of days to get here. Then
we'll hang this killer.'

Lucy Bracken looked at Clancy with eyes
that had lost all hope. He had had many
black days since that first day he had set eyes
on Lucy in the Bracken yard. But none as
black as the one he was now living through.

CHAPTER FOUR

Jack Stone slammed the cell door shut on Dan Clancy, and then took the marshal's oath of office in the presence of Ned Drucker and two of his fellow Town Council members, with a smirk that left no one in any doubt but that the oath of office meant nothing to him. Lance Roebuck had been angling for a long time to get his man as marshal, and the thorn of Sam Brody out of his side. Clancy thought that it was mighty convenient that Roebuck's plans should have come to fruition, hitch-free. But voicing such an opinion when it seemed that everyone, particularly those packing a clout in Watts Bend, would be as useless as trying to grow corn on a boulder. Dan Clancy figured that now, with Sam Brody out of the way, there was nothing to prevent Lance

Roebuck from making Watts Bend an open town with him as the lord of all he surveyed.

Nathan Roebuck, Lance Roebuck's uncle, was failing by the day, and soon the cattle empire which he had built would pass to his late brother's son and his only heir. Already, Lance Roebuck was letting it be known to his neighbours that he would be extending the boundaries of the Roebuck ranch. And he was also letting it be known that he was not prepared to let any man stand in the way of that expansion. Every day new faces were turning up at the ranch, men who were not sure which end a cow had her tail; men who had no business being anywhere near cow country. The way they wore their guns was a certain pointer to their true profession.

As his uncle Nathan's health took turn after turn for the worse, Lance Roebuck had been steadily building himself a small army. Already, some of his neighbours seeing the writing on the wall were making plans to up and leave, ready to accept the way below par price that their ranches were worth, rather than run the risk of bucking Lance Roebuck with all the dangers that resistance would entail. There had, in the recent past, been a litany of poisoned water-holes and mysterious fires and accidents to encourage compliance with Roebuck's wishes.

In time town and range would wake up to Roebuck's true nature. However, Dan Clancy reckoned that by then Lance Roebuck would be too powerful a monster for anyone to do anything about.

'You know, Lance,' Stone said, 'I figure that it would be a pure waste of a judge's time to haul him all the way here, when that bum Clancy is guilty anyway. I reckon we should just drag him out of here to the nearest tree and save a whole heap of trouble not to mention expense, like grubbin' Clancy and payin' Judge Fleming's expenses.'

Ned Drucker glanced anxiously to the council members who had accompanied him as witnesses to Jack Stone's swearing in as marshal. He found no backing there.

'You've got a point, Marshal Stone,' Lance

Roebuck intoned, letting his gaze slide Drucker's way. 'But you're working for the town now, Jack. And I reckon that Mr Drucker, being the Town Council chairman, might have something to say about your proposition. Ned?'

'Well...'

'Well, what?' Stone harangued the dithering chairman.

'Let the man gather his thoughts, Marshal,' Roebuck rebuked Stone. 'You take all the time you need, Ned,' he added generously. 'Only thing is that I don't want to be still standing here in my old age,' he laughed.

Stone laughed with him. The men with Drucker joined in. Ned Drucker tried to smile, but all he could manage was a bunching of his facial muscles.

'Well,' he began again, even more ponderously than he had previously, 'I think that the law might have a problem with hanging a man without due process, Marshal.'

'I am the damn law!' Stone exploded.

'Yes, M-Marshal Stone,' Drucker stammered. 'What I mean–'

Lance Roebuck interjected: 'What Ned means, Jack, is that a town with a prosperous future on the cards, must be seen to be law-abiding and proper in its treatment of all citizens, even no-good curs like Dan Clancy. Ain't that so, Ned?'

'Surely is, Lance,' Drucker eagerly agreed.

'We'll wait for the judge,' Roebuck concluded.

'You're the boss, Lance,' Stone said.

Roebuck shot his hardcase a villainous look.

'Not anymore I ain't, Jack,' he growled. 'You work for the town now. As marshal, Ned Drucker is your new boss.'

Realizing his blunder, Jack Stone quickly agreed with Roebuck.

'Sure Mr Drucker is the boss,' he said.

'And I guess we'd best all make tracks and let you get on with all that paper work that's necessary for a hanging,' Roebuck said. 'But though you're now the marshal, Jack, don't you forget your old friends and become a stranger at the ranch.'

'I surely won't,' Stone said, openly scoffing at Drucker and his partners. 'I reckon I'll often drop by for the benefit of your wisdom, Lance. And I reckon that you'll make a fine and upstanding jury foreman when the time comes. Ain't that so gents?' he asked the Town Council members.

Enthusiastically nodding heads was the response to his suggestion.

'Anyway I can serve, you just let me know,' Lance Roebuck said expansively.

Roebuck ushered Drucker and his colleagues out of the marshal's office ahead of him. He paused before he joined them, exchanging a knowing glance with Jack Stone, the import of which was not lost on Dan Clancy. He'd never stand trial, he figured that a lynch rope would be his lot, or maybe a bullet in the back while supposedly escaping.

Just as Lance Roebuck was pulling the door shut behind him, it was flung open again and Lucy Bracken swept into the law office.

'Why, hello, Lucy,' Roebuck greeted affably. 'You look a picture, but that's nothing new, is it. You've always looked prettier than a spring flower.'

Lucy pointedly ignored Lance Roebuck's presence, and his compliment. She addressed Stone: 'I've come to visit with your prisoner, Marshal.'

'Visit?' Stone snorted. 'Why would you want to waste your time visiting a dead man, Miss Bracken?'

'The prisoner and Lucy have their rights, Marshal,' Roebuck said stonily.

Chastized, and not liking it one little bit, Stone grunted grudgingly: 'Five minutes. No more.'

Lance Roebuck tipped his hat to Lucy and made to depart.

'Why don't you drop by the ranch for Sunday lunch, Lucy,' he invited. 'That would sure please me.' Then pointedly: 'And your ma too, I reckon.'

'I'm a big girl,' Lucy flung back. 'I make up my own mind on the company I keep, Lance.'

'Don't reckon that your ma would want you hobnobbing with a killer,' was Roebuck's parting shot.

Denied the opportunity to respond, Lucy instead shot Jack Stone a malevolent glance.

'I'd prefer my conversation with Dan to be private, Marshal,' she grated, as Stone went to accompany her to Clancy's cell. 'So if you'd be kind enough to remove yourself to the other side of the door, I'd be obliged.'

Jack Stone seemed set to ignore Lucy's request until she said:

'I'm sure that Lance would agree.'

Grumbling, Jack Stone did as Lucy requested.

'It sure is awful when a killer's got all sorts of rights that make no sense at all, if you ask me.'

'No one is asking you, Stone,' Lucy said sharply. Pulling up a chair close to the cell, she enquired concernedly of Clancy: 'Are you OK, Dan?'

Clancy shook his head. 'As much as a man facing a noose can be, Lucy.'

'You didn't murder Sam Brody. Did you, Dan?'

'Do you believe that I did, Lucy?'

'No!'

'Doesn't sound like that to me, asking the question you just did.' Lucy averted her gaze. 'If you don't believe me, they might as well hang me right now. What hope do I have of anyone else believing me if you don't, Lucy?' he said dispiritedly.

CHAPTER FIVE

On seeing the ocean of hurt in Dan Clancy's blue eyes, Lucy quickly apologized.

'I'm sorry, Dan. Of course you didn't kill Sam. Why would you. He was the only man in town who would have anything to do with...' She chewed off her words.

'With a drunk, Lucy,' Dan said.

Lucy sprang off her chair.

'My being here is doing you no good at all, Dan.'

Impulsively, he reached through the bars of the cell and grabbed hold of her hands as she turned to leave.

'Your visit's the best thing that's happened to me today, Lucy,' he said sincerely. Tears welled up in Lucy Bracken's eyes. 'Hush now,' he coaxed. 'Ain't nothing to be gained by tears.'

'Oh, Dan,' she wailed. 'Why didn't you just keep on riding that day you passed the house.'

'And by now you'd be Mrs Lance Roebuck, I guess. And I guess Lance wouldn't be hellbent on trouble if, as you say, I had kept on riding.'

'You didn't push Lance in the direction he's gone, Dan.'

'He was in love with you, Lucy. He took your refusal to marry him badly. That started the canker of badness now driving him. No denying that.'

'Lance is a grown man and responsible for his own ways,' Lucy pronounced. 'I wouldn't have married him anyway. Even if you'd never stopped by the house.'

'That ain't true. Everyone says that before I showed up, it was taken for granted that you'd be Lance Roebuck's wife.'

'Well everyone isn't always right!' Lucy declared.

Clancy's gaze drifted to some distant point.

'Funny, ain't it,' he mused. 'If I'd taken a different trail that day, the one that passed behind your house through the hills for instance, we both would have had different lives. I wouldn't have met Sarah Browne, and you'd be Mrs Lance Roebuck.'

Dan Clancy's face took on the dreamy look he got when he thought of Sarah Browne.

The wind whipped up a fiercesome dust cloud. Dan Clancy rode with the brim of his hat low on his forehead to prevent his eyeballs from being worn raw in their sockets. His stay in Watts Bend had not worked out as he had hoped it would. With no chance of work in the offing, he had decided to ride out. Besides, he figured that with Lucy Bracken's rejection of Lauce Roebuck's proposal of marriage, and the common perception being that her refusal was down to his presence in Watts Bend, there was no future for him in that town.

He heard the crack of splintering wood first, before he spotted a woman stranded in the creek, the left-sided wheel of her buggy shattered. Observing that the swift-flowing creek, swollen by recent rain, was threatening to upend the buggy, Dan hurried to the woman's assistance, taking her in his arms to safety just before a log rammed the vehicle.

He had been pleased to find that the woman's initial stiff reaction to the liberty he had taken had, by the time he had reached the bank of the creek, melted away. And he flattered himself that the woman might have preferred if the creek had been twice the width it was.

'Thank you, sir,' she said. 'Most chivalrous of you.'

Dan Clancy, a man who had long ago lost his shyness, found himself blushing as he took the woman's proffered hand in his to shake. Her hand was soft and warm, and lingered in his for a mite longer than it might have, he flattered himself.

'My name is Sarah Browne,' she said.

'Ah...' Dan found himself tongue-tied. 'Dan Clancy,' he had finally managed to get out in a funny, strangulated voice.

'It seems that I'll be looking for a ride home,' Sarah said. 'Would you oblige?'

Dan Clancy wondered if he might have died, and this was an angel guarding heaven's gates.

'Be glad to, ma'am,' he said with an eagerness which obviously pleased Sarah Browne.

'Ma'am,' she chuckled. 'Do I look that matronly?'

'No!'

'Then please call me Sarah. And I shall call you Dan. Agreed?'

'Yes, m– I mean Sarah.'

'Good. Then if you'd be so kind as to help me on to your horse, we can set out for my home, Dan.'

Clancy was intrigued by Sarah Browne's accent which he could not place, though he had travelled far and wide over many territories.

Settled upon his horse, and loving the soft warmth of her body pressed against his, he had asked: 'From these parts, Sarah?'

'Dear me, no. I'm from a place called Merrivale-on-Severn.' And in an amused response to Dan's raised eyebrows, added: 'England.'

The remainder of the short journey to Sarah Browne's house was a pleasant, often humourous trek, that had Dan Clancy mourning its end. When Sarah invited him inside, he recalled how he had never dismounted from a nag faster. That was the start of a three-month stay at Merrivale Cottage; three months in which he had done the chores and repairs, while Sarah Browne finished the book she was writing about an *hombre* called Inspector Devizes – a Scotland Yard *bobby* who was in fact an English lord.

'A *bobby?*' Dan had questioned Sarah.

Sarah had laughed heartily.

'A kind of marshal without a horse and sixgun,' she explained.

It was during that bout of rockabye laughter that Sarah had fallen into his arms, and he kissed her for the first time. She had kissed him back with no less a passion, and after that there was no going back to being host and guest.

'Maybe,' Sarah Browne had said, when it seemed that they could not live under the same roof without somehow ending up entangled, 'we should go and see the minister in town, Dan.'

Clancy raised no objection. Because she had said what he had been trying to work up the courage to say. After tying the knot that same day, Sarah and he had had six weeks of indescribable happiness before Sarah fell from a stallion she rode out on each morning, broke her neck and died. On hearing the news, distraught, Dan Clancy had finished a bottle of whiskey to ease his pain. Only the pain always returned and Dan took more liquor and in ever greater quantity to ease his anguish, until the need to quench his thirst overrode every other consideration, even his grief for Sarah.

When Dan came from his reverie, Lucy had left. Jack Stone had followed her outside.

69

'Why're you wasting your time on a no-good like Clancy?' was his question. 'When any day of your choosing you could walk into the Roebuck parlour and make it your own.'

Lucy Bracken's first reaction was one of anger, until she realised that Stone's enquiry was couched in terms of utter puzzlement. And she had to admit that, to anyone else, hers was the carry on of a complete fool. Lance Roebuck was the territory's most eligible man, good-looking, too. How could anyone understand why she should pine for a man who did not have two dimes to rub together, and who spent his time chasing his next drink.

'You know, Marshal,' Lucy said, her spirits at rock bottom. 'Some things are just plain darn inexplicable.'

Stone watched her walk away, scratching his head. He returned inside the jail and took to scrutinizing his decrepit and ragged specimen of a prisoner. His puzzlement deepening, he scratched his head even more.

The following morning, handing charge of Dan Clancy over to a trusted town crony, Jack Stone rode out to the Roebuck ranch. On arriving, Lance Roebuck joined him and they rode into the hills. Because Roebuck's business with his appointee marshal was of a kind that was best not overheard.

'What do you want done with Clancy, Lance?' Jack Stone asked, when the paranoid rancher finally drew rein.

Slyly, Roebuck pondered: 'How many prisoners do you reckon try to bust out of jail, Jack?'

'Plenty, I guess,' was Stone's cagey reply.

'Well, just let's say that you had a jail-break. You'd have every right to try and prevent that break-out, wouldn't you?'

Catching the drift of Roebuck's thinking, Jack Stone grinned and said: 'Sure would, Lance.'

'Such an eventuality would save all those questions that might come up at a trial, don't you think?' Stone nodded in agreement. 'Folk have long memories. And they might just wonder why you and me slipped out of the saloon last night.'

'No one saw us,' Stone asserted.

Lance Roebuck snorted. 'Can you be absolutely certain of that, Jack?'

Jack Stone rubbed a sudden sweat from his brow.

'As sure as I can be, Lance,' he mumbled, and added: 'And that ain't good 'nuff, is it?'

Lance Roebuck shook his head.

'With Brody's murderer wormfood all those questions that might arise won't be asked.'

Stone rowed in whole-heartedly behind Lance Roebuck's pact of murder.

'You'd best get back to town now,' Roebuck said, his devilry completed. 'Telegraph for that judge.'

'Telegraph? Why?'

'Because it must look like the wheels for a fair trial have been set in motion, that's why,' he snarled impatiently. 'Folk might wonder why you hadn't sent for the judge. And they might start asking a whole pile of awkward questions when a convenient twist of fate sees off the need for a trial.'

'You're worryin' 'bout nothin', Lance,' Stone said. 'No one will do nothin' to upset the cash from the Roebuck ranch jangling in their tills.'

'Why take the chance on someone getting a conscience,' Roebuck grated. 'You just do as I say, and we'll both be OK.'

Pointing his horse towards town, Jack Stone said: 'You're the boss.'

He was a little way off when Lance Roebuck called: 'And don't you ever forget that, Marshal Stone.'

CHAPTER SIX

When Stone arrived back in town, he headed straight for the telegraph office and sent a wire to Judge Rupert Stockton Fleming in Kiowa Falls, requesting his attendance to preside over a murder trial. When handing over the wire to the telegraph clerk, Stone shrewdly laid the groundwork for Dan Clancy's pre-trial demise as planned by Lance Roebuck.

'Hope that judge don't take too long, Larry.' Stone planted the seed which would blossom into Clancy's murder with the telegraph clerk and others present. 'Clancy's a desperate man. Got nothin' to lose, seein' that a noose is a certainty.'

The wizened clerk responded in exactly the manner Jack Stone had hoped he would.

'You expecting trouble, Marshal?'

'Wouldn't surprise me none,' Stone said. 'Like I said, Clancy's got nothin' to lose.' He sighed as if the world had just been placed on his shoulders. 'I can tell you good folk, that I won't rest easy 'til the judge arrives and that cur Clancy gets the justice he deserves at the end of a rope.'

One of the telegraph's customers, a middle-aged woman, clutched at the pearl necklace she wore and said: 'I never thought that Dan Clancy was a killer. It came as a dreadful surprise to me. Why, I used to hire him to do some chores now and then. Outside the house, of course. Couldn't have him in the house, now could I.'

'No, ma'am,' was Stone's reply, his nose twitching as if picking up a bad smell.

'Imagine,' the woman fretted. 'At any time he might have murdered me, too.'

'A man with a thirst like Clancy's sometimes goes loco,' Stone said. 'I reckon that's what happened last night. Denied the bottle of rotgut Brody gave him, Clancy must have had the devil's own thirst. Figured that he'd head for Sam Brody's to scrounge a drink, the late marshal being kinder than most folk to him. When he got there, I guess Brody turned him away and Clancy went crazy and killed him.'

He snorted.

'Kinda funny, don't you think? If Sam Brody had not intervened in Lance's fun and games, Clancy wouldn't have had that godawful thirst. And Brody would still be alive.'

He shook his head mournfully. He was joined in his head-shaking by the telegraph clerk and his customers.

Jack Stone left the telegraph office, job well done, he reckoned. Turning in to the marshal's office, his thoughts were darker than the darkest night.

'No need to fatten him up, Barney,' Stone railed on entering the jail and seeing the sizeable lunch before Dan Clancy, presuming it was his stand-in who had provided the prisoner with the feast. 'Keep grubbin' him like that, and there won't be a strong enough rope to hang him with!'

'Ain't m' doin', Jack,' Barney grumbled. 'Lucy Bracken it was who brung Clancy his lunch.'

Stone snarled: 'That woman must be plumb out of her skull to be moonin' over a dead man. When there's a real live one like Lance Roebuck yearnin' for her.'

'Beats ev'rythin', don't it,' the stand-in gaoler mused. 'Guess the man who can understand women ain't been born yet, Jack.'

When they were alone, Clancy said to Stone: 'Enjoy your ride out to the Roebuck ranch?'

Taken aback, Stone protested: 'I ain't been an'where near the Roebuck ranch, Clancy.'

'The red dust on your Levis says different,' Clancy observed. 'That's Roebuck range dust.'

Jack Stone hurriedly brushed off the reddish dust, claiming: 'This whole territory's got the same dust.'

'No it ain't, Marshal,' Stone's title was delivered with biting sarcasm. 'The dust you're skinning your hands trying to rid yourself of, is peculiar to a basin on the Roebuck spread. Something to do with an ore mine that was once there.'

'Aw, shut your gob!' Stone barked. 'I've got more to do than listen to your ravin', Clancy.' He grinned evilly. 'Like arrangin' your hangin'.'

Shrewdly, Clancy guessed, 'Is Roebuck afraid that the judge will ask too many embarrassing questions, if I get to stand trial?'

Despite his effort to ignore Dan's speculation, Stone was unable to resist probing: 'What kinda questions would they be?'

'Oh...' Dan tossed his head as if to clutch inspiration from the heavens. 'Maybe questions like what you and Lance Roebuck were doing at Sam Brody's house last night.'

Jack Stone's Adam's apple bobbed.

'Lance and me were nowhere near Brody's house last night,' he said, his eyes shifting away from Clancy's sceptical gaze.

'You see, Stone,' Dan continued. 'Roebuck

knew that I'd be at the marshal's house early. He heard me promise Sam in the saloon last night. He could murder Sam, and then turn up on cue this morning to rope me in for his killing with your help. Which makes you every bit as guilty as Roebuck is.'

Dan Clancy held Stone's eyes fixed.

'If he hangs, you'll swing too.'

Fear haunted Jack Stone's eyes. 'Ain't no one goin' to hang 'cept you, Clancy.'

Up to that point, Dan Clancy had only been fishing. But he now knew by Stone's nervous reaction that he had landed the biggest fish in the pond. He had had his suspicions that Lance Roebuck's hand was at work somewhere in the terrible deeds of the night before, but now those suspicions had turned to certainty.

'You must not give up, Dan,' Lucy had urged when she had delivered his lunch to the jail, finding Dan in low spirits.

'I'm on my way to the gallows for sure, Lucy,' he'd said despondently.

'Are you going to accept hanging just like

you've been accepting every other darn misfortune?' Lucy retorted angrily. 'If you are, then I guess the sooner it's done with the better.'

'Why do you persist in trying to save me from myself, Lucy?' Dan had asked.

'If you don't know why by now, Dan Clancy,' Lucy trumpeted. 'Then I'd be wasting my breath trying to get it through that granite block you call a head.'

Lucy Bracken's dressing down had sparked his spirits. When she had left he cleared the fog from his brain, and as it lifted, Sam Brody's probable killer had come into view. His role as the stooge who would conveniently hang for Sam Brody's murder became clear. And Jack Stone's reaction to the scenario he had outlined, confirmed the veracity of his thinking.

However, his problem now was that he could do nothing about it. He was the town drunk. Lance Roebuck would, with his uncle failing by the day, soon be one of the territory's most powerful and richest men.

And he was in jail.

Dan Clancy knew that the odds were stacked sky high against him.

CHAPTER SEVEN

Clancy watched Jack Stone get increasingly edgy. And when he showed any sign of relaxing, Dan cleverly stoked his fear again.

'Roebuck ain't going to wait for a judge and a trial. Is he, Stone?' Clancy prodded.

'I sent a wire to Judge Fleming,' Stone railed. 'He'll be here in no time at all.'

'A bluff,' Clancy said. 'Roebuck's idea to go through the motions, I reckon. That way no awkward questions would be asked when I don't make it to the gallows.'

'Shuddup your yapping!' Stone snarled.

'It's got to be Lance Roebuck's thinking, I figure. You're not smart enough, Stone.'

Enraged by Clancy's insult, Stone drew his sixgun and charged to the cell. Clancy stepped back from the bars, fearing that he might have prodded Stone too far. The

Roebuck appointee had a flash temper that had more than once overrode his good sense. Not that stepping back into the cell would save him. Stone was at the cell door, his emotions roller-coasting. Clancy had no doubt that Jack Stone would have liked to blast him, but he was hoping that Lance Roebuck's tutoring would prevail. If he was to be killed before he got to the gallows, his demise would have to be in a fashion that would not cause concern to a maverick citizen who might ask questions. There were a few who had not been inveigled by Lance Roebuck's largesse, but would they have the courage to quiz Roebuck should it be necessary to do so? Dan Clancy thought: either way, if he was a harp player it would not make a damn jot of difference to him.

Several gunshots rang out which diverted Stone's attention. The sound of shattering glass and a brawl had the lackey marshal heading for the door. Relieved that the immediate danger to his well-being had passed, Dan drew breath again. The sounds of the ruckus faded, and minutes later the jail door opened and Stone shoved an ill-tempered, russet-haired youngster the worse for liquor in ahead of him, the youngster fighting him every step of the way. Stone threw the youngster's pistol on the desk, grabbed a bunch of keys and frog marched him to Clancy's cell.

'There's three empty cells,' Clancy complained, shuddering. In the last couple of minutes the whiskey demon inside him had come alive, and the last thing he needed was a liquored up kid adding to his misery.

Stone scowled. 'Why dirty-up perfectly good cells with like trash,' he barked.

The youngster gave the scruffy and ragged Dan Clancy the once over and snorted. 'You ain't in no position to object, if I was a mangy dog, mister. And,' he growled at Stone, 'Mr Roebuck ain't going to like his new top gun being thrown in jail.'

'Roebuck. Top gun?' Stone yelped.

'Das right,' the youngster slurred. 'I'm Junior Bellew, Marshal.' The colour drained from Stone's face and left in its wake a grey, sweaty visage. 'My brothers Frank and Ike ain't going to be too impressed neither! If I was you, I'd be gone long before they arrive, lawman.'

'Have they been hired by Lance Roebuck, too?' Stone asked, his jaw on his chest.

'Sure have,' Junior Bellew confirmed cockily.

Stunned both by the news that Lance Roebuck had imported a top gun, a position which he himself figured he filled in the Roebuck set-up, and the revelation that he had slung in jail one of the meanest killers in the West with all the dangers that could follow such a brash action, Jack Stone dropped his guard. With the speed of a polecat, from his right boot a knife flashed in Junior Bellew's hand and slashed Stone's side. Shocked, Stone staggered aside, grabbing the cell bars for support as he slid to the floor. Contemptuously, Bellew followed through with a kick to Stone's stomach.

'Coming, mister?' Bellew asked Clancy,

striding ahead to the desk to collect his gun. He turned to look at Dan, still trying to grapple with the violence he had witnessed. 'Stay an' rot if you want. But it don't make any sense with the door wide open.'

Dan Clancy had but a second to make up his mind. Remaining in jail would rob him of any chance he might have to clear his name. And, of course, in a week or so he'd be hanged. He hurried after Junior Bellew. They were at the door when Jack Stone's gun exploded. Junior Bellew arched, his hand clutching at his back. But Stone's bullet had already exploded out of the gunfighter's chest. Bellew toppled on to the boardwalk, dead. Dan leapt over him and vaulted into the saddle of the first horse hitched to the rail outside the marshal's office. The confusion gave him the seconds he needed to gallop out of town. As he reached the end of Main, guns behind him were opening up. Thankfully, the horse he had stolen was sturdy of limb and strong of wind. He had been lucky that the men who had been close at hand when he had busted out of the jail, had chosen to use their guns instead of their heads. The lost time before they vaulted in to the saddle gave Clancy a good head start, and he knew the country well. Most of the men who would form the posse would be townies; fellas who had not ventured far beyond the town boundaries in years. Their unfamiliarity with the rocky terrain into which Clancy rode would work to his advantage. With luck he'd outride them. But he knew that he would be far from safe. Because as soon as news of the happenings in town broke, a Roebuck outfit would be in the saddle, and their knowledge of the terrain would not be found wanting.

Panic gripped Dan. He was in poor physical shape for a long period of posse dodging. And the demons of thirst were tormenting him. His shakes were becoming so bad that he was barely able to stay in the saddle. And they would get much worse. So would his thirst. When that happened, he knew that his only concern would be to quench that thirst, even if it meant risking his very life.

Bent over in the saddle, Clancy headed into the hills, and not solely to evade the posse. Bantry O'Shea, a crusty Irishman from a place called Bantry in County Cork, lived in the hills where he brewed the sweetest moonshine that a man ever tasted. Just a couple of slugs was all he needed to see him right, Clancy lied to himself. As his torment increased, the horse he was on was pretty much left to finding its own path. An hour on, Dan had the worse shakes he had ever experienced. The terrain around him spun out of control and his bones rattled as he fell from the saddle. He curled up, unable to go any further.

CHAPTER EIGHT

The rider going hell for leather was hailing the Roebuck ranch house long before he leapt from the saddle, his momentum forcing Lance Roebuck to grab the youngster as he shot past.

'It's Jack Stone, Mr Roebuck,' the messenger from town said, winded. 'Killed a man. Got cut up bad though.'

'What man?'

'A stranger. Youngster. And Clancy's busted outa jail too.'

'Youngster? Stranger? What happened?' Lance Roebuck's questions were delivered quick-fire in a low, shaky growl. He was uncaring of how badly hurt his henchman was. His only concern was how the events in town would effect him.

'Louie Cassidy, he owns the saloon,' the

young man unnecessarily informed Roebuck, much to his annoyance, 'says that the fella shot was none other than Junior Bellew.' Lance Roebuck's mouth became as dry as the Mojave at high noon. 'But heck that can't be. I mean what business would the likes of Junior Bellew have in our neck-o'-the-woods, Mr Roebuck?'

'Was Stone still sucking air when you left town?'

'Last I heard, he was. But Doc Albright was working real hard to keep it that way.'

'This Bellew *hombre* was shot by Stone?' Roebuck quizzed urgently. 'How come? Bellew is one of the fastest guns, and one of the wiliest coyotes around.'

'Junior Bellew, if what Louie Cassidy says is true, was causing a ruckus in the saloon. Jack Stone arrested him and hauled him off to jail, and then–'

'Stone hog-tied Junior Bellew?' Lance Roebuck interjected in awe.

'Got the drop on him. Came in the back way. The marshal had a gun in Bellew's spine before he knew it.'

Roebuck snorted. 'Didn't realize that Jack had as much smarts as that. What happened then?'

'Well, that ain't none too clear, Mr Roebuck. All we know is that Jack Stone is cut up and bleeding like a pig. And Junior Bellew got backshot, just as he was bustin' outa jail.'

The messenger scratched his head.

'Still can't figure out what a gunnie like Junior Bellew was doing in town. How do you figure it, Mr Roebuck?'

'Passing through I guess,' Roebuck muttered evasively. He took a ten-dollar bill from his pocket and gave it to the youngster. 'I appreciate your bringing the news so fast, boy,' he said.

The messenger's eyes went saucer-wide on seeing the money.

'I ain't never afore had a whole ten dollars all at once,' he said, stunned by his good fortune.

'Saddle my horse,' Roebuck told a nearby

rannie, and announced: 'I want twelve hard riding men mounted and ready in five minutes, to hunt down this wildcat killer Clancy.'

'Ain't you going to town to see Jack Stone?' the youngster asked. 'Get the facts.'

'Git, boy!' Roebuck growled at the messenger.

'Yes, sir, Mr Roebuck!'

The youngster was in the saddle and galloping off before Lance Roebuck drew another breath, clutching tightly to the ten-dollar bill in his fist.

Before mounting up to lead the posse, Lance Roebuck had a hurried conversation with a trusted hardcase, an albino called for some perverse reason, Blackie Blake. After the posse departed, acting on Roebuck's instructions, Blake made tracks for town.

As night closed in and the dangers of the unfamiliar terrain mounted, the hastily convened town posse lost its grit for the pursuit of Dan Clancy. The collective wisdom was that Lance Roebuck would hunt the town drunk to ground and hang him where he found him. Some of the men, eager to ingratiate themselves with Roebuck, headed off to tie up with the Roebuck posse. The remainder returned to town, and were glad when they reached the safety of its environs unharmed.

Dan Clancy teetering on the brink of collapse had watched the town posse come closer. Unable to continue on he had resigned himself to capture when, only feet from where he lay in hiding, the posse turned tail. He had figured them correctly when he had reckoned that they would soon lose their appetite for the chase, when a bed on stony ground in dangerous country was near at hand. But it was with no great relief that Dan watched them ride away. He might even have welcomed being hauled back to town for the chance of getting a whiskey inside him to ease his torment. He also knew that the next posse that would show up, the Roebuck posse, would stay in the saddle until they ran him to ground. Spending most of every day in the saddle, their butts would not be as tender as townies' behinds. And weak as he was, his progress could be matched by a snail.

When a shadow crossed over him, Dan Clancy reckoned that trouble had already come a-calling. He turned slowly. Sudden movement was never wise when a man crept up behind you, because he did so for a reason.

'You look done in, fella,' said the burly man holding a blunderbus on Dan.

Clancy's relief was intense. Bantry O'Shea had put on poundage since he had last crossed paths with him, but there could not be another man in the West with such red hair and an even redder beard, though flecked now round the mouth with grey.

'That about hits the nail on the head sure enough, Bantry,' Dan said.

The Irishman came a few paces closer to study the skulking man. When he finally recognized Clancy, though he tried, there was no stopping his jaw dropping open.

'Dan Clancy?' he asked, still not wholly certain that he was addressing the right man.

Three years previously when Clancy had last met up with Bantry O'Shea, while passing through the hills on his way to Watts Bend, he had been a well-muscled, spritely man, with eyes that were a clear blue and not the unhealthy yellow of a man who had punished his liver with rotgut.

'It's me all right, Bantry,' Dan confirmed sadly.

'What the hell happened you?' the Irishman asked bluntly. And then seeing the shudders gripping Clancy he knew.

Ashamed, Dan turned his face away.

'Was that posse chasing you, Dan?' the moonshiner enquired. Clancy nodded.

'What for?'

'Murder.'

'Mur–You ain't no killer,' he said positively.

'No I'm not, Bantry. But back in Watts Bend, you'd not find a soul who'd agree with you.'

Moved by Clancy's dejected demeanour, Bantry O'Shea said: 'I guess I'd best get you indoors, Dan. Get some grub in you. Then we can jaw.'

The plea in Dan Clancy's eyes was unmistakable, and instantly recognized by the moonshiner.

'OK, friend,' Bantry agreed. 'A little moonshine, too. But only a little.' Clancy's tongue licked parched, cracked lips. 'Can you get on your nag? More important, can you stay on?'

'As I recall, it isn't far to your cabin,' Dan said. 'I'll hang on.'

'Let's get going then. I've seen other riders.'

'They'll be the Roebuck outfit.'

'Old Nathan Roebuck still alive?'

'Just about.'

Mounting up, Bantry opined: 'A good man, Nathan. Only he ain't in the saddle looking for you. Who would that be?'

'That would be Lance Roebuck, Nathan's nephew and only kin.'

Riding up the hill trail to his cabin, the moonshiner shrewdly queried: 'Is this Lance Roebuck *hombre* part of your problem?'

'More than part,' Dan Clancy said bitterly.

'They look like men who won't give up easily,' the Irishman observed.

'They won't,' Dan confirmed.

'Looks like we've got a whole lot of talking to do, Dan.'

Lance Roebuck sat grim-faced in the saddle, a worried man. The last thing he had wanted was for Dan Clancy to be on the loose, talking. His mind went back to two nights previously and how his anger had simmered and finally reached boiling point at Sam Brody's intervention on Clancy's behalf. For some time he had watched Brody's growling determination to rein him in. It was the worst kept secret in Watts Bend, that the marshal had been continuously harping at the Town Council to draw a line in the sand. He had not worried about the council doing so. The council consisted of businessmen who were growing fat on the business they transacted with the Roebuck ranch. And that business could only grow as the ranch expanded, which he intended fully that it should. He had not set any boundaries, because he knew that there would be none. He intended to grab every blade of grass, and had arranged for the Bellew Brothers, the most ruthless enforcers a man could employ, to *persuade* his neighbours to accept his miserly offer and move on. But he'd have no qualms about burying them right where they were, if that's what it took. His uncle had protested his methods and ambitions, but he had ignored him. Lance Roebuck saw the old man as a burden and an impediment to his ambitions. He had decided that if Nathan Roebuck did not oblige and die soon, he'd help him on his way to those greener pastures he was always yapping about.

It was a stroke of bad fortune that Jack Stone had slung Junior Bellew in jail, and it had been a miscalculation on his part not to have informed Stone of the gunfighter's impending arrival in town. But the youngest Bellew had arrived a couple of days earlier than planned. And if he had told Stone of his plans to import gun-talent, it would have put his nose out of joint, seeing that Stone reckoned that he was to be the top Roebuck henchman when he forced his neighbours off the range. And he had needed Jack Stone sweet-humoured, until his plan for Dan Clancy's demise had been completed.

Now he was left with a mountain-high mess that needed sorting fast, before Frank and Ike Bellew skinned him alive. Jack Stone was his man, and therefore the Bellews would hold him to account for Stone's actions. Lance Roebuck shivered as if he were buck naked in the middle of a Yukon winter.

The close friendship of the three brothers was well documented, and he did not have enough cash in the bank to compensate Frank and Ike Bellew for their kid brother's demise. So his normal means of skirting trouble, would not apply.

There was only one compensation that

would satisfy the outlaw brothers, and that was an eye for an eye. He had to point the outlaws in another direction – Dan Clancy's direction. Stone would already be dead, because he had dispatched Blackie Blake to kill him. With Stone silenced, that would leave Dan Clancy as the perfect stooge to hang the blame for Junior Bellew's murder on. Clancy could easily be painted as a wild-cat killer (he'd have no problem providing witnesses to that fact if necessary), who had already murdered a benefactor in Sam Brody. Raising the idea that if he murdered one benefactor, he could do so again, should not be too difficult. He was already in the frame for Sam Brody's murder. So with a modicum of luck, two birds could be killed with the one stone. And if he played his cards right, Lance Roebuck reckoned that he might end up the hero instead of the villain, by delivering up to Frank and Ike Bellew their brother's killer – dead, of course.

That was why he had to find and kill Dan Clancy, pronto.

CHAPTER NINE

Blackie Blake hitched his horse and made his way through the dense undergrowth to the creek where he had heard voices. Having covered a lot of country during his outlaw days before Lance Roebuck had hired him, he had developed an ear for the way a man delivered his lingo, and he reckoned that the men now speaking were Texans or as near to the Lone Star state as did not matter. Before he got a glimpse of the grubbing men, Blake figured that their identity would come as no surprise to him. One of the men was lanky and as lean as a piece of string, with a dark scowling countenance that often frightened men more than the low-slung Colt he wore. The second man had more beef on him. His visage was that of a preacher. This would be Ike Bellew, the deadlier of the duo, because he smiled and was mannerly right up to the second he killed you. Frank Bellew was, despite his Satanic appearance, less of a killer. The difference between the brothers was slight, but at least with Frank Bellew a man would think before he challenged. Whereas with the saintly-looking Ike Bellew, there was no hint of the evil within him until it was way too late. Mostly the Bellew Brothers rode together, always Frank and Ike. But Junior Bellew, the youngest by ten years, had a rebellious streak that sometimes saw him ride alone, but never too far ahead of his brothers should their help be needed. And it was Junior Bellew who was the meanest of the three, having at just twenty years old as many notches on his gun as he had lived years. Some would say that there should have been a lot more. That the twenty notches represented only men whom Junior had considered worthy of recognition as being close to equals in depravity. There was, folk said, a whole army of lesser men whom Junior Bellew had killed for fun, or out of sheer bad-temper.

'Junior should've long since been back from that look-see in Watts Bend,' Frank Bellew said restlessly, throwing the dregs of his coffee on the fire.

Ike Bellew was untroubled.

'Junior's prob'ly in some dove's drawers, Frank,' he said, grinning lecherously. 'Lucky bastard!'

Frank Bellew began to pace, mumbling: 'Junior's got a thing 'bout time-keeping, Ike. Got it from our pa. Pa used to watch time like a miser watches dimes. Many's the whipping he handed out for just being seconds late,' he added bitterly, obviously having been on the receiving end of his father's wrath many times.

'Pa had a godawful temper, sure enough,' Ike Bellew granted his older brother. 'And he hated you something awful, Frank.'

'Figured I wasn't his,' the senior Bellew said. 'Told me so just before he died. Hope he's rotting in hell. But I doubt if even the devil would have him!'

'You mean Ma...?' Ike Bellew considered the implications of what Frank had revealed, and concluded: 'I'll be damned.'

'Pa said that she had a fling with a rangy Virginian who he hired as a jack-of-all-trades, him having busted his leg felling a tree for winter fire.'

Ike Bellew sniggered.

'Sure took his work serious if he laid Ma. Musta known after the first ten seconds of making Pa's acquaintance, that he'd kill him for even sniffing near her. Pa would kill you for stealing a fist of beans, let alone poking his woman.'

'Pa knew where the Virginian had been and what had happened when Ma started to show signs of her philandering. He took off faster than a bullet. Didn't matter though. It took Pa a whole year to find him, but when he did that Southern gent met his Maker with a lot less than his Maker had given him starting out.'

Ike Bellew chuckled.

Frank added: 'Pa said that Charlie Lafont's

real punishment was that he'd spent all of eternity with all o' them angels, and he could do nothing 'bout it but look.'

Ike Bellew joined in his brother's laughter. When their laughter faded out, Ike Bellew studied Frank and said a tad critically, 'Ya know, Frank. That explains why you always looked so diff'rent to me an' Junior.'

Ike's observation was about as pleasing to Frank Bellew as a brothel to a eunuch. He glared malevolently at Ike who, quickly, on seeing the elder Bellew's temper rise, apologized. Ike was not sure if Frank would kill him, but he was not going to take the chance on calling it wrongly.

After grim consideration of Ike before he accepted his apology, Frank kicked dust on the fire and growled, 'I gotta bad feeling about Junior. Let's ride.'

Ike Bellew dragged himself lazily from his sitting position against a tree trunk. 'Junior's well able to look after hisself, Frank. He's faster than you and me put together.'

'Stop your griping,' Frank Bellew snapped. 'Who's the boss of this outfit an'way?'

'You are, Brother,' Ike said, with just the right amount of malice, tempered with the right amount of bonhomie to make a man wonder if he had been complimented or insulted.

Undecided, but vain enough to accept Ike Bellew's honey and gall comment as a compliment of sorts, Frank Bellew mounted up and rode ahead of Ike along the creek, his mood dour. Catching him up, and observing his mood, Ike asked, 'You really figure that Junior's got hisself in a tangle, Frank?'

Ike had seen Frank Bellew's uncanny knack of sensing when Junior had bitten off more than he could chew.

'Mebbe,' he murmured. 'But if an'one's harmed Junior, he'll wish that he'd never been born. And that goes for an'one of his harmer's friends too.'

Blackie Blake gulped. He had set out from the Roebuck ranch ready to do Lance Roebuck's bidding. But now, having overheard Frank Bellew's dire prediction, he was having second thoughts. The outlaws would have expected Junior to have Lance Roebuck's protection. The fact that Junior had arrived in town unannounced and bucking for trouble, would be conveniently forgotten in their rage. Watts Bend was a Roebuck town and therefore, as they would see, the responsibility for Junior Bellew's safety would rest squarely with Lance Roebuck. And the Bellews' fight would be with any man who served Roebuck. The chances were that their killing spree would never reach him, Blake hoped, but the question now was should he gamble on that, or...?

The hill trail, as Dan Clancy was seeing it, had a thousand times more twists and turns in it than there really was. The trees bordering the trail were leaning towards him, to his mind, threatening to crush him. And they were taking on the oddest shapes, all twisted and menacing. Observing the signs of alcoholic hallucination, Bantry O'Shea took hold of Clancy's reins and led him. The final stretch of trail to his cabin skirted a deep ravine, and the slightest misjudgement by Clancy would pitch him headlong into it. Bantry rode ravine side, ready to grab Clancy should the need arise.

'I ain't a damn kid!' Clancy growled with drunken garrulousness, trying to grab his reins back.

The moonshiner held on firmly to them.

'You're in no fit state, Dan,' he stated bluntly. 'And you either do things my way, or we part company right now.' Though suffering the fires of hell in his belly, Dan Clancy still had sense enough to know that should the Irishman abandon him, he'd be finished. He relented on his struggle for the reins. 'That's better,' Bantry said. 'Now grab that saddlehorn and hold on tight.'

The ravine swam up to meet Clancy, its rocks and boulders spinning wildly. The Irishman, an experienced hill-rider, guided, coaxed and scolded Dan along the trail. They successfully, if scarily, negotiated the narrow track, and it was with relief that the moonshiner helped Clancy dismount on reaching the cabin safely. He helped his hunched and quaking visitor inside, and placed him on the only bunk the cabin had.

'Lie still,' he ordered Clancy, whose thrashing about was reaching a peak as his craving for liquor reached the unbearable. 'I'll be right back.'

Clancy grabbed the Irishman's arm, his tormented eyes pleading with him. 'Just one drink, Bantry.'

'When I come back, maybe.'

Clancy tugged him back when he tried to leave.

'Just a sip, then?' The moonshiner hesitated. 'For pity's sake, Bantry,' Clancy pleaded.

'OK,' O'Shea conceded. 'Just a mouthful, mind.'

The Irishman went to a press and took out a bottle of moonshine. He poured enough just to cover the bottom of a glass and handed it to Dan who gulped it down, shuddering as the fiery liquid exploded in his craving gut.

'This I'm taking with me,' Bantry said, when Dan Clancy's eyes became fixed on the bottle. He tucked the bottle inside his shirt.

Outside, the moonshiner broke off the branch of a sapling and retraced the trail he and Clancy had traversed. Going back over a mile, walking on the stony edge of the trail, as best he could he brushed it free of sign. Satisfied that he had done all that he could to obliterate their sign, he returned to the cabin to face what would be an ordeal. Because he had decided that the best favour he could do Dan Clancy was to starve him of liquor for as long as it would take to break its hold on him. All Clancy could ever do was manage rather than overcome his thirst; liquor to most men was a pleasure to be partaken of on occasion. But to other less fortunate men, once snared by liquor, it was a curse that bedevilled them to their grave.

Back in Watts Bend, Lucy Bracken was both elated and troubled. She was over the moon that Dan Clancy had, at least for the time being, evaded the hangman, but concerned that the stories about the break-out from the jail, should Dan be apprehended, would only serve to speed his appointment with the gallows. She could not believe that Dan would shoot a man in the back, even the kind of man that Junior Bellew was. And why would he, if it was Bellew who had made the break-out from his incarceration possible?

And then there was Sam Brody's murder.

To her shame, she had momentarily questioned Dan's assertion of innocence. How could she have doubted Dan. If she had stopped to rein in her panic, she would have realized that of all the men in town, Sam Brody would be the last man whom Dan Clancy would harm. Not that Dan was a violent man anyway. Marshal Brody, rest his soul, had always been considerate and kind to Dan. Up to the very night he was slain, stepping in to stymie Lance Roebuck's humiliation of him. A terrible thought surfaced in Lucy Bracken's mind; a thought so black that she immediately shunned it. But despite her best efforts, the dreadful thought persisted. Knowing the Lance Roebuck of the past, her dark thoughts were utterly without merit. But the Lance Roebuck of the past was light years away from the present Lance Roebuck. And, contrasting the two, the idea that Lance might harm Sam Brody in a fit of spite was, Lucy depressingly concluded, not beyond the bounds of possibility. His opportune appearance at the scene of the crime, might very well have been designed to rope Dan in for Brody's murder. Roebuck was privy to the arrangement Sam Brody had made with Dan the previous night, and would have known of Dan's appointment at the Brody house. However, convincing as her theorising was, for that's all it was, Lucy was loath to think of Lance Roebuck as the cold-blooded monster he would have to be to kill a man on the flimsy slight Sam Brody had given. She was ready to dismiss the idea out of hand. But the thought that Lance Roebuck now, was light years away from the kindly man she was on track to marry before Dan Clancy arrived on the scene kept nagging, refusing to let her mind rest.

Lucy, though long since having ruled Dan out as Brody's killer, could plainly see how a jury could be swayed by Lance Roebuck's assertion that Dan, driven by thirst, had gone to the marshal's house to bum a bottle. That they had argued, and that Dan, desperate and driven, had struck out at the marshal. Putting herself in a juryman's place, asked to decide between the stories of a town drunk and one of its leading citizens, Lucy saw no contest. Even if Watts Bend was not a Roebuck town to begin with.

Rattled, Lucy reacted ungraciously to the sound of the shop doorbell. The last thing she wanted was another dressmaking chore. She had her hands full already, and was way behind due to the turmoil of her emotions. She swung around, ready to refuse any new custom.

'Ma,' Lucy said in total surprise.

'Good Lord, girl,' Martha Bracken said.

'That face would frighten Satan himself.'

'Sorry, Ma,' Lucy quickly apologized.

'That's OK. I guess your nerves are a little raw, Lucy.'

It was Martha Bracken's first visit to Lucy's shop since she had opened for business two years previously. She had left home at the tail-end of a long line of arguments with her ma about her continued hope that Dan Clancy would look her way. It had been a bitter parting. And both women, sharing a common stubborn streak, had not had the mettle to set aside their injured pride and mend bridges. And, Lucy realized, it was no credit to her that it was her mother who had had the courage to put her pride aside.

Martha Bracken glanced about the neat and colourful shop. The evidence of a full order book was apparent in the rolls of cloth being readied for working on.

'You've done well, Lucy,' was Martha's conclusion, voiced with no small amount of pride.

'Thanks, Ma,' Lucy said. 'It's sure nice

that you've come to visit.'

'Been meaning to. But I wasn't sure that I'd be welcome.'

Lucy raced from behind the counter to embrace her mother, gently scolding her, 'That was darn foolish thinking.'

'Your pa said that I was a stubborn old fool.' Martha grinned. 'Take that smug look off your face, girl. Pa said the same about you, without the *old* bit. You got your pa in a whole heap of trouble, young lady. Him sneaking in to see you whenever he was in town. And then trying to cover his tracks when I darn well knew what he'd been up to.'

Her grin exploded in a hearty laugh.

'When it comes to old fools, your pa's cornered the market!'

Her curiosity piqued, Lucy asked, 'How did you know?'

'Your pa kept wandering home with pieces of thread all over him. For a spell, I thought that he might be dallying with another woman. Your pa is about that age, when men get to doing silly things. But knowing your pa, I figured that he'd curb any such notions. So that only left one reason for those fancy threads and snippets of cloth.'

'Your ma would borrow the devil's tail to whip me with, if she caught me out in a whopper,' her pa would say. *'Your ma reckons that if you're let be, your head will clear and you'll stop all this foolishness about Dan Clancy and marry Lance Roebuck as was always planned.'*

'That hobo Clancy will break your heart, Lucy,' her ma had predicted. *'You'll see.'*

Martha Bracken's prediction had come heartbreakingly to pass, when Dan had married another woman. Grasping his chance, Lance Roebuck had proposed.

'Only a woman with rocks inside her head would refuse,' had been her ma's fiery outburst when Lucy had done just that.

Lucy had steadfastly clung to the hope, as the lovelorn do, that soon Dan would realize his mistake and turn to her. Instead cruel tragedy struck, and Dan had tried to drown his sorrows instead of sharing his woes, and had begun his slide down the slippery pole into daily oblivion as a way of dealing with his pain. While all the time Lucy had grappled with her overwhelming sadness, not understanding how Dan Clancy couldn't see that no other woman in God's creation could love him more than she did.

The heady euphoria of her ma's visit abating, Lucy asked quietly, 'Why've you come, Ma?'

'Not to gloat, if that's what you're thinking. Even though Dan Clancy has turned out to be more of a no-good than I could have imagined.'

'Dan's not a bad man, Ma,' Lucy said, jumping in to defend Clancy. 'Just an unfortunate one,' she added sadly.

Martha Bracken's sigh was long and weary.

'Still hankering after him, though he's a killer.'

'Dan's no killer, Ma. And if that's what you truly think,'– Lucy marched to the door and flung it open – 'I believe you've outstayed your welcome.'

Martha Bracken stood stock still, her eyes taking in every inch of her angry daughter. 'I had to find out if you still thought the same way about Dan Clancy, before I told you that I don't believe for one minute that he's a murderer. A hobo, yes. A drifter, yes. A drunk, definitely. But,' she shook her head vigorously, 'not a killer.'

'Oh, Ma,' Lucy said, relieved. She hugged Martha Bracken.

'That's not to say that I've changed my mind about you and him, Lucy,' she stated. 'I still think that you should tie the knot with Lance Roebuck.'

'Ma, Lance is not the Lance you knew.'

'Fiddly!' Martha Bracken dismissed. 'Don't you understand, Lucy? It broke Lance's heart when you took to mooning over Dan Clancy, and there was no talking sense to you.' Martha held up her hand to stall Lucy's comments. 'Lance came round to the house and told me so himself. Told me clear out that there was nothing worth having or living for without you, girl. That your rejection of him ripped the heart right out of him. I figure that if you were to–'

'Never knew that Lance felt that strongly, Ma.'

'Well, now that you do, what're you going to do about it?'

Lance Roebuck, wearing a worried frown, drew rein and stretched in the saddle. The fingers of night were stretching across the hills to clutch the sunset away. Frank Dawson, now hoping to be Jack Stone's replacement as top dog, came alongside him.

'Clancy can't have vanished into thin air, Lance,' he said.

'We've been all over these damn hills,' Roebuck snarled. 'Not a darn sign.'

'Clancy's a drunk. Likely that he fell off his nag into a ravine.'

'Then where's his horse?' Roebuck quizzed.

'Probably gone with him,' Dawson reasoned.

Roebuck considered Dawson's theory, but rejecting it he concluded, 'He's got to be somewhere in these hills. In his condition, Clancy wouldn't have the spit to ride far.'

Frank Dawson became thoughtful.

'You know...'

Roebuck barked, 'I won't unless you tell me!'

'Well, I've been thinking. What's the most important thing in Clancy's life, Lance?'

'Whiskey,' Roebuck said without hesitation.

'Yeah. Whiskey. And what do you find in the hills. Moonshine.'

Roebuck's spirit bucked up.

'You're right, Frank.' Then, somewhat deflated, his eyes searched the hills in the gathering gloom. 'But there could be a million stills. And you'd probably never find a single one.'

Dawson said, 'We could start with the Irishman. An *hombre* called Bantry O'Shea.' He licked dry lips. 'Brews the sweetest mountain dew you'll ever sup. And if Clancy's not there, I reckon that with a little persuasion, O'Shea will point the way to the other stills.'

Lance Roebuck's grin was a smug one.

'You know, Frank. You're a real smart fella,' he complimented. 'So what're we waiting for?'

'Better to wait for first light now,' Dawson counselled. 'These trails ain't the same at night as they be by day. I reckon we should set up camp, and not risk injury to man or beast, Lance.'

Dawson's suggestion did not rest easy with Roebuck. However, he soon saw the good sense of his henchman's caution.

'Camp, it'll be,' he said.

High in the hills, Bantry O'Shea shuffled between the bunk he had Dan Clancy tied to, and the cabin door from where he scanned the darkening trail leading to the cabin for any sign of riders. He knew that he had done a good job in obliterating the evidence of his and Clancy's passing, but he also knew that there was no way that a man could completely do so. A good tracker would pick up on something as small as a broken twig. He also knew that trackers of that skill were not as plentiful as snowflakes in a snowstorm, but there were one or two in the territory a man with the clout of a Roebuck could hire.

His other problem was Clancy's hellish wailing and moaning as his body fought his whiskey-fever. With night creeping in, sound would carry a whole lot further.

'Just one drink, Bantry,' Clancy pleaded for the umpteenth time.

And the Irishman answered for the umpteenth time, 'There's no such thing as one drink for a man with liquor-sickness.'

'You don't have the right to put me through this hell,' Clancy argued. 'A man can make up his own mind the way he wants to die.'

At the end of his tether, after many hours of nursing and arguing with Clancy, Bantry had almost cut the ropes and given him a bottle, just for the sake of peace and quiet. But just when he might have given way, he thought of the man Dan Clancy had been the times he had passed through the hills on his way to some place or other, searching for the ever-elusive el dorado he was looking to settle in. That bright-eyed and bushy-tailed man had become lost inside the shivering, whimpering shell of a man Clancy had become, and he held firm against Clancy's ranting and cursing.

However, he still had not decided what he would do when the posse, probably a Roebuck gang, showed up. Would he be willing to protect Clancy at the risk of losing his own life? The moonshiner shivered. He was not a brave man. In fact, if truth be known he lived in the solitude of the hills because he did not feel safe in the bustling danger of a town or city. He figured that his fear of so-called civilization was born one winter's day in his home town of Bantry in County Cork. A horse fair was in progress, and with it came the tribes and the inevitable clashes accompanying such gatherings. One such clash, right in front of him, when a man was stabbed in the throat in a dispute over a couple of pence, had had a profound effect on him. He had been ten years old. And from that day forward he had always been wary of any place where there were crowds.

As the last threads of daylight surrendered to the night, Bantry closed the cabin door, reckoning that danger would not now come before morning. Dan Clancy had, thankfully, stopped his ranting and had fallen into a restless, exhausted sleep. O'Shea hoped that it would be a long sleep.

Blackie Blake had tracked Ike and Frank Bellew to within sight of the town's lights, tossing in his mind whether he should risk making their acquaintance, or give them a wide berth and do Lance Roebuck's bidding. There were several trails into town which he could have used that would have had him in Watts Bend long before the Bellews put in an appearance, to deal with Jack Stone. But evesdropping on Frank and Ike Bellew's fireside jawing had posed a dilemma for him. Should he stick with

Roebuck, who might not be around for long if the Bellews decided that he had not offered their kid brother the protection they would have expected him to provide? Or should he attempt to throw in his lot with the outlaws? The Bellew trio used to be a quartet. A couple of months previously they had lost their fourth man, a cousin, in a bank raid on the Mexican border, and had not replaced him. And now with Junior Bellew's demise, they were two men short. Maybe, he was thinking, that if he were to give them the full gist of what had happened to Junior Bellew, pointing the finger directly at Lance Roebuck by way of his choice of Jack Stone as marshal, he just might end up replacing Junior. He had grown weary of nursing cows: he had remained on at the Roebuck ranch in the hope that when Lance Roebuck locked horns with his neighbours, he'd become one of his top guns and benefit from the rich pickings range-wars brought. But with Roebuck having decided to import gun-talent, the prospect of rich pickings was likely up in smoke.

Maybe, Blake thought, he might embellish the story he would tell Frank and Ike Bellew. Tell them that he had overheard Roebuck tell Stone that he had changed his mind about hiring them. That when they showed up Stone should throw them in the slammer. They'd surely hang, and that would be that. When only Junior showed up, Stone, not the brightest wick in the West, had acted on Roebuck's orders. Only the plan went haywire when Junior Bellew got the drop on Stone.

Mulling over his plan, Blackie Blake picked up his pace to close the gap between him and the outlaws, should he finally decide to spin the yarn he had concocted.

Lucy Bracken had accepted her ma's invitation to supper, and was now ensconced in the parlour with her pa, digesting a fine meal.

'What is it, Pa?' Lucy eventually asked, growing uneasy under Hank Bracken's steady gaze.

Hank lit a pipe and drew deeply of the tobacco before revealing what was on his mind.

'Ma says that you're still pining for this feller Clancy. That so?'

'My head says that I shouldn't be,' Lucy said wearily. 'But my heart just won't listen to my head, Pa.'

'Life with Lance Roebuck would sure be a whole lot easier,' her pa counselled.

'Yes, it would,' Lucy agreed.

'You'd want for nothing.'

'Only the man I truly love, Pa.'

Hank Bracken considered his daughter for a long spell, before saying, 'I reckon I know where Dan Clancy is hiding out, Lucy.'

Lucy's heart staggered.

'There's this Irishman in the hills south of town, a feller called Bantry O'Shea. Brews fine moonshine. The last time I visited to replenish my stock, he was asking about Dan. Clancy had spent a couple of weeks in his company on his way here: helped him to build a new cabin. Bantry reckoned that Dan Clancy was a right honest sort of fella.'

He looked Lucy squarely in the eye.

'So do I, Lucy,' he stated.

'Are you saying that I should go to Dan, Pa?'

'I guess that's what I'm saying. And I reckon that it's high time you told him straight out that you love him more than any other man alive, too.'

'But he must know that, Pa.'

'Knowing it, and being told so, are different things, Lucy. Might not make an iota of difference. But at least it will clear the air between you two.'

'Ma will hit the roof, Pa.'

The parlour door opened and Martha Bracken stepped into the room. Lucy tensed, expecting herself and her pa to be fiercely rebuked. But what Lucy's ma had to say came as a complete surprise to her.

'Your pa is right, Lucy. It's time to put your cards on the table, girl. I won't deny that I'm hoping that Dan Clancy will send you packing, and that then you'll settle for Lance Roebuck. And maybe, eventually, all this bad blood between Clancy and Roebuck that's at the root of most of the trouble round here will at last be purged.'

Ecstatic, Lucy sprang out of her chair.

'How do I find this Bantry O'Shea, Pa?'

'I'll take you to him,' Hank Bracken said.

Lucy went to the room door, where she paused.

'Well, what are we waiting for, Pa?'

He grinned. 'First light.'

'First light,' Lucy agreed, truly happy for the first time in a long time.

CHAPTER TEN

Dan Clancy's eyes shot open. He held his hands up to ward off the demons chasing him from his nightmare. He cried out, thrashing about. Bantry O'Shea held him down until he calmed, and Dan's eyes shed their terror. During the night, when Clancy had slept, Bantry had undone the ropes he had had to tie him down with.

Clancy calmed, the Irishman offered, 'I've got fresh coffee brewing. Want some?'

'Coffee,' Clancy murmured, his eyes fixed on a bottle of moonshine on the table, his mouth full of sand. His swollen tongue filled every inch of his mouth and more.

Bantry looked at the bottle.

'Moonshine, too,' he said. 'If that's what you *really* want, Dan.'

'If it's all the same with you, Bantry,'

Clancy stood up on legs that were as steady as a feather in a gale, 'I'd surely prefer moonshine.'

The Irishman stepped aside to allow Clancy a clear passage to the bottle of mountain dew. O'Shea had long ago learned that the only time a man quit drinking was when he was good and ready to, and not before. That was the thing with liquor-fever. A man either got the will to quit, or lacked the will and killed himself. And preaching sobriety was just a sheer waste of a man's breath.

Clancy grabbed the bottle of moonshine and held it to his parched lips, already anticipating the warm relief that would flood through him when the liquor reached the pit of his stomach. Suddenly he stayed his hand, a little of the liquor spilling down his shirt front, the smell of the moonshine wafted into his nostrils, and filled him with a longing that bordered on pure insanity.

'What're you waiting for?' Bantry said. 'You've got a bottle. Oblivion ain't far away.'

Dan again raised the bottle to his lips, his hand shaking. Once more he hesitated to drink.

'There's still that fresh coffee, Dan,' Bantry invited kindly.

Clancy slammed the bottle back down on the table and collapsed on to a chair. The moonshiner, not showing any emotion, positive or negative, poured the coffee and sat at the table, letting the stillness of the morning act as a balm. After a time, he said:

'You smell something awful, Dan. There's a tub out back that you might want to use. Soap, too.'

Clancy at first took umbrage, but then sniffed at himself and cordially conceded: 'Yeah. Maybe I'll soak at that, Bantry.'

A while later, scrubbed, Dan came back to the cabin to dress. Bantry had clean trousers and a shirt laid out on the bed.

'No point in scraping all that dirt off, if you're going to get into the same duds,' he said. And a minute later, looking at Clancy dressed in clothes that were several sizes too big for him, Bantry added: 'I've put on a coupla pounds in recent times.' Then, chuckling, 'Maybe a mite more than a coupla pounds.' He went to the door. 'I've got some chores to do. If you want, you can help out, Dan.'

Bantry left, leaving the bottle of moonshine on the table, figuring that if Dan resisted the urge to guzzle when he was alone, there might just be a glimmer of hope that he could begin to live life again without the crutch of a bottle.

Dan sat looking at the bottle of moonshine for a long time. A thick, oily sweat covered his body from his toenails to the roots of his dark hair. His heart pounded, fit to leap right out of his mouth. Inside his head were the dark whisperings of temptation. His innards curled up and hurt. His hands and legs shook, and his breath was as tight in his chest as the fully wound spring of a clock. The bottle of moonshine swam towards him, sometimes only inches away from his touch.

Lance Roebuck paced edgily as his men prepared to break camp, anxious to reach the moonshiner's cabin which Frank Dawson had spoken of. He was conscious of time ticking away. He wondered if Frank and Ike Bellew had arrived in town. He fretted that Jack Stone might be still alive and able to talk. Having gone behind his back to hire the Bellews, Stone would be sour. He was a man scorned, with a lot to tell. Stone was right there in the room when he had killed Sam Brody. Maybe no one would believe Stone, if he did talk. But then again, someone might. Blackie Blake was a proficient killer, but Lance Roebuck had a sense of things not going according to plan.

'Unnecessary worry,' was Dawson's opinion, when Roebuck had voiced his fears. 'Blackie knows who puts dollars in his pocket. Besides, Stone was probably already dead when Blackie reached town,' he reasoned. 'Knife wounds bleed a lot, and it's hard to stem the flow.' Mounting up, he concluded: 'I'd prefer to be gunshot any day to being cut.'

Grimly, Lance Roebuck said: 'I have a preference for neither myself.'

Blackie Blake decided to hedge his bets. Picking up his pace, he reached town ahead of Frank and Ike Bellew by way of a little-known trail that, due to the danger of rock falls, was only used by men wanting to stay out of sight for one reason or another.

On reaching town, with time short, Blake did not waste a second. He immediately made his way to the rear of the doc's office where his infirmary was. He edged up to a lighted window and cautiously peered inside. There were three beds in the infirmary but only one patient – Jack Stone. And he looked a long way from being dead. In fact he looked quite pecker. And now that Blake had confirmed that Stone was sucking air, his choice was clear. He could slip through the window and do as Lance Roebuck wanted. Or he could try to cut a deal with Frank and Ike Bellew.

Lucy Bracken was exhausted. She hadn't slept a wink, eager as she had been to be up and away. Lack of sleep and the rigours of the hill trails had taken their toll. Hank Bracken had had to draw rein several times, slowing their progress. In the distance, a half-hour previously, they had caught sight of a band of riders.

'The Roebuck posse, I reckon,' had been Bracken's conclusion. 'But they're looking on spec,' he had told a worried Lucy. Not having the heart to tell her that their direction was taking them straight to Bantry O'Shea's front door. But they had the edge on the Roebuck posse, and could travel quicker than a big body of riders. Still, Bracken reckoned that the Roebuck horses would be better fed and more used to the hilly terrain than the flea-bitten nags he and Lucy were riding.

And Lance Roebuck did not have a woman in tow to worry about.

Perched on a boulder that provided him with an eagle's view of the trails through the hills, O'Shea had his concentration interrupted by the sound of breaking glass. He stood on top of the boulder for a clear view of the cabin. Dan was standing on the cabin stoop, bleary-eyed but sober. He reckoned that Dan had overcome the temptation that was standing on the table when he had left, and that the glass he had heard breaking was the bottle of moonshine. He'd still be a long way off of going an hour without liquor, but Clancy had made a start. And a good start at that.

CHAPTER ELEVEN

'Howdy, Dan,' Bantry greeted when Clancy put in an appearance, and with a wry grin added: 'You still look like something the cat dragged in, but there's hint of colour in your cheeks and a perkiness in your step and eyes.'

Dan sat on the boulder alongside the Irishman, and looked at the myriad of trails winding up through the hills, much of them cutting through trees that would offer approaching riders good cover. Understanding Dan's concern, which he shared, the moonshiner said with a confidence he was far from feeling: 'We'll spot any intruders well in advance, Dan.'

'No we won't, Bantry,' Dan replied. 'And even if we did, there wouldn't be much we could do about it.' He held out shaking hands. 'I'd be more likely to shoot myself than anyone else.' He settled his gaze on the Irishman and stood up. 'And you don't owe me anything, Bantry. I'll saddle up and ride out.'

O'Shea laughed heartily.

'Did I say something to amuse you?' Dan asked tetchily.

'With the breath you've got, your nag would be blind drunk in no time. Prob'ly go loco and jump into a canyon or ravine.'

Clancy flinched.

'Don't take umbrage,' the moonshiner said. 'The reality is, Dan, that you're in no fit condition to go anywhere.'

It was the truth and Clancy knew it.

'A coupla weeks, maybe. If you stay liquor free.' O'Shea fixed Clancy with an unflinching eye. 'Now I'll put my cards on the table. I'm not sure yet how I'll react if a shooting or hanging posse shows up. I might stand squarely against them. On the other hand, I might figure that it would be a pure waste of a fine figure of a fella like me to exchange lead with a posse. If you hang 'round, that's a chance you'll have to take, Dan.'

Bantry resumed his perusal of the hills.

'Knowing all the facts, you make up your own mind, friend.'

Dan's mind went back to three years previously when, having spent an amiable sojourn with the moonshiner on his way to Watts Bend, the Irishman had generously offered him a partnership.

'Sure is peaceful in these hills,' he had told him. 'They might just be the el dorado you're chasing, Dan.'

'Don't think the smell of timber in my nose all the time is my cup of tea, Bantry,' Dan had said. 'Fact is I need the noise and bustle of a town to relax me.'

They had let the matter rest there, neither man wanting to offend the other by his views on their respective ways of life. But now Dan could not help but wonder how fate might have treated him, had he accepted O'Shea's offer. But then, he consoled himself, he would not have met Sarah Browne, and he would not have had those happy times with her. Regrettably brief as his time with Sarah had been, they had been golden hours that had he his time to live over, he'd willingly and knowingly pay again the terrible price he had paid since her tragic passing.

And had he accepted Bantry's offer, he would not have met Lucy Bracken either. And if Martha Bracken had looked more kindly on him than she had, Sarah Browne would never have entered his life. Because Lucy would have long before he crossed paths with Sarah, been his wife. He reckoned that his days with Lucy, had fate dealt him that hand, would have been every bit as happy as his time with Sarah Browne had been.

Dan hadn't moved one foot beyond the other, when Bantry O'Shea invited:

'Why don't you sit your butt on this boulder and keep watch, while I brew a pot of coffee.' He handed over his rifle to Clancy.

Dan chuckled.

'Right now, if a rider comes up the trail,

I'll be seeing ten of him, Bantry.'

The moonshiner laughed along with Dan.

'Shoot the bastard in the middle,' he said.

'Why the fella in the middle?' Clancy enquired.

Bantry O' Shea shrugged. 'You gotta start somewhere, don't ya.'

Dan Clancy handed his rifle back to O'Shea.

'I'll brew the coffee, Bantry,' he said. 'Safer that way.'

Dan walked off towards the cabin. As he passed a scraggy stand of timber, thinned by a recent storm, Lance Roebuck caught sight of him, and snatching his rifle from its saddle scabbard, the more wily Frank Dawson stayed his hand.

'You'll need the devil's own luck to down him from here,' he placated an angry Lance Roebuck. 'And if you missed, he'd know we were at his front door.'

'I still ramrod this outfit, Dawson,' Roebuck growled. However, after a short, sullen silence, Roebuck conceded Dawson's point.

He spurred his horse forward up the winding trail. Dawson again risked his boss's wrath.

'We ain't been spotted yet. But I figure we should creep from here on in.' He soothed Roebuck's angst at losing face with his men. 'I know this country well, Mr Roebuck. There's a high perch near the cabin from where a man could see clear to Mexico. I figure, Clancy coming from that direction, that there's a look-out on that perch.'

He looked to the tree-clad hills.

'Use the cover of the trees,' he counselled. 'No time at all, we'll be knocking on Clancy's door.'

'Clever *hombre*, ain't you,' Roebuck snorted. 'But don't you ever get too clever for your own good, Dawson,' he warned. 'Dismount,' he ordered his men.

CHAPTER TWELVE

Nearing Bantry O'Shea's cabin, Hank Bracken suddenly grabbed his daughter's reins and steered her into the trees.

'The Roebuck outfit,' he explained, pointing to the riders lower down, Lance Roebuck seeming to be in dispute with a man Hank Bracken knew as Frank Dawson; a man whom he reckoned was as dangerous as a spitting rattler.

'Why are they dismounting, Pa?' Lucy asked.

Hank Bracken's worry deepened. He knew why they were dismounting all right. They planned to creep up on Bantry O'Shea's cabin. And that meant that they had a darn good reason for their caution. O'Shea's cabin was only round a bend in the trail a little further on, but a straight stretch of sparsely covered trail lay between them and that bend. They would almost certainly be spotted by the Roebuck outfit. There was a canyon that would bring them out on the blind side of the cabin, but he would have to backtrack aways to take that route. He did not see any other way of reaching the cabin safely. And there was no way that he was going to risk Lucy's safety in any lead-slinging contest.

'Come on.' He hauled Lucy after him.

'Why are we back-tracking, Pa?' she questioned. 'You said that we were near Bantry O'Shea's cabin.'

'Don't argue,' Hank Bracken scolded his daughter. 'Just darn well do as your pa tells you to.'

All he could hope for now was that Roebuck and his cronies' necessarily cautious approach through the trees, would take more time than his route to the moonshiner's cabin.

Just outside of Watts Bend, Frank and Ike

Bellew drew rein on seeing the road blocked by an albino. Force of habit had their hands dropping to their guns.

'Easy, fellas,' Blackie Blake said in a friendly tone. 'I mean you boys no harm.'

'You're lucky you're not already dead, mister,' Frank Bellew said icily.

Blake tightened his stomach muscles to check the rumble in his bowels.

'Lost your tongue?' Ike Bellew snarled, his hand a claw over his sixgun.

'No, sir,' Blake said. 'I'm here to warn you boys about trouble ahead.'

'Trouble?' Frank Bellew's eyes narrowed, as did his mouth.

Blackie Blake tried to swallow, but had not the saliva to do so.

'Junior's dead,' he blurted out.

Frank and Ike Bellew's eyes bored into Blake, sucking energy from him until he became so limp that he was forced to grab his saddlehorn to remain in the saddle.

'If you've got a story to tell, tell it!' Frank Bellew growled.

Dan Clancy blinked, rubbed his eyes and blinked again. Lucy Bracken was still there, beckoning to him from behind a woodpile at the rear of the cabin. Her pa was there now too! Best ignore the vision, he reckoned. He'd have many such hallucinations as he dried out.

'Dan.'

'Lucy? Is that really you?' Clancy asked in disbelief.

'Get out of sight, Dan,' Lucy called urgently.

Lance Roebuck had Clancy in his sights.

'Maybe you shouldn't have your name on this bullet, Mr Roebuck,' Frank Dawson slyly suggested. 'Lucy Bracken's hatred for the man who'll kill Clancy will last to her grave, I reckon.' Roebuck immediately got the drift and sense of Dawson's reasoning. Dawson boldly took the rifle from his employer's grasp. 'Lucy can hate me all she likes, Mr Roebuck.'

Frank Dawson clapped himself on the back. He had played his cards well. He had deftly leaped to the top of Roebuck's coterie of henchmen. In a couple of seconds, when he killed Clancy, his position as top dog in the Roebuck outfit would be secure.

Dawson's finger squeezed the Winchester's trigger.

CHAPTER THIRTEEN

A volley of shots, from somewhere above and behind the cabin, pinned down the Roebuck men, forcing Dawson to shoot wildly. The spitting lead compelled Lance Roebuck to dive for cover in a head-over-heals leap that mimicked a circus clown's antics, bringing a smile to some of the men, before two of them folded. Then the smiles changed to snarls.

Dawson, though joining in Roebuck's ungainly scramble, saw Clancy drop. When he checked from cover a moment later, Dan had not moved. His bullet had been wild, but lucky.

Hank Bracken dragged Lucy back, as she struggled to reach Dan. Harshly, he told her: 'It's no good, Lucy. Dan's beyond help now.'

Dawson, spotting Hank Bracken's struggle with Lucy, nudged Roebuck.

'Hold your fire, you idiots,' Lance ordered, as Roebuck guns opened up. 'You'll hit Lucy!' Crouched behind the cabin, Lucy and her pa heard Roebuck's offer: 'You and your pa can ride out, Lucy. I mean you no harm, though you clearly came to give succour to that cur Clancy.'

Lucy's response was vibrantly defiant.

'Then you're going to have to kill me, Lance. Because if you don't, I'll give witness to the act of cold-blooded murder you committed or had a hand in.'

'Murder? We're a posse hunting down a mad-dog killer, Lucy,' Roebuck called back.

'You're nothing but a bunch of murdering henchmen.' This opinion was venomously delivered by Hank Bracken. 'Dan Clancy didn't stand a chance! That makes his killing murder, plain and simple. I'll see you swing for murder, Roebuck.'

Hank Bracken took his now sobbing daughter in his arms.

'Hush, girl,' he coaxed. 'You did your best.'

'Dan's dead,' she grieved. 'And that means that I'm dead too, Pa.'

On the ridge behind the cabin, Bantry O'Shea was taking advantage of the exchanges between Roebuck and the Brackens to reload his rifle. His spirits were low, because when he used up the bullets he had, that would be that. He cursed, too. He had got involved in a fight that was nothing to do with him.

'That's gone and torn it, Bantry!' he rebuked himself. 'Moonshine's your business. Not trading slugs. Now that you've dropped two Roebuck men, he'll want his revenge.'

He could take comfort in the fact that he had done the decent thing by coming to the aid of helpless folk. But all that was left now was the hope that when he cashed in, the good Lord would not be too harsh in his judgement.

The Irishman surveyed the terrain leading to the ridge. There were a hundred ways to flush him out. His chances were zero.

Frank and Ike Bellew heard out Blackie Blake's much embellished and untruthful version of Junior Bellew's demise; of how Lance Roebuck had changed his mind about hiring the Bellews, and how he had arranged Junior Bellew's killing.

'The plan was to let Junior bust out of jail. Then Stone, Roebuck's man, would shoot Junior in the back.' It pleased Blake to see Frank and Ike Bellew's anger rise in ratio to his vivid description of what he conveyed as an insider's account of Lance Roebuck's back-stabbing, as overheard by him. 'Junior was shot down like a mangy dog,' he finished, fervently shaking his head at his supposed incomprehension of the foul act of murder which had been perpetrated.

Frank and Ike Bellew's towering rage had been exactly what Blake had hoped for. Because anger scattered a man's common sense, and put the need for revenge paramount to all other considerations, like picking holes in his tall yarn. Blake, who had in his years of skullduggery become an accomplished and slick-tongued liar, took pride in the exercise of a skill which had got him out of many a tight corner.

'Roebuck's scheme didn't exactly work out as planned, though. Junior cut Stone pretty bad. But he's still sucking air in the town infirmary, should you want to drop by.'

'Obliged, mister,' Frank Bellew said, his tone hollow. 'But what I want to know is, why you risked telling us.'

It was time to play his trump card.

'I figured that if I did you boys a favour, you might be of a mind to return one.'

'What kinda favour?' was Ike Bellew's snarling question.

'That when you leave, I'll ride out with you.'

'We don't ride with no strangers,' Frank Bellew said. 'It's always been kin.'

'You're a man short since that cousin of yours was shot down in that bank raid near the border a coupla months ago,' Blake croaked, praying that he was not being too pushy. 'And now with Junior gone too...'

Frank Bellew stayed Ike's rejection of Blake.

'The man's got a point, Ike,' he said. 'We'll need a man to fill Junior's shoes for that railroad heist we've been planning. But after that we'll see,' Frank Bellew cautioned Blake.

'That's good enough for me,' Blake agreed, eagerly.

'What's your handle?' Frank Bellew asked.

'Blake. Blackie Blake.'

Observing Blake's albino appearance, Ike Bellew laughed.

'Blackie?' he snorted.

'My pa, the drunken old bastard, had a strange sense of humour,' Blake said sourly. 'Hope the devil's burned him long ago.'

'Having a side-winder like you for a boy, I guess the devil owned your pa right from the cradle,' Ike Bellew opined.

'Guess so,' Blake said, laughing along with the outlaws while raging inside.

Laughter done with, Frank Bellew said: 'You can ride with us, Blake. But not only when we leave town. Right now.'

'Now?' Blake questioned, shakily.

'Got a problem with that?' Ike Bellew growled.

Blackie Blake shook his head vigorously.

'No, sir,' he quickly assured the outlaws.

However, his immediate inclusion in the gang posed a problem. He had hoped to lie low until the Bellews had done their killing and were ready to leave town. The last thing he wanted was to be caught in the middle of a shooting war, where he could end up on the receiving end of punishment whichever side won. Lance Roebuck would, in no time at all, become aware of his treachery. And there was the risk that should Roebuck get a chance to talk to Frank and Ike Bellew, they just might begin to mull over the tall tale he'd spun them. Sweating under Ike Bellew's beady-eyed glare, Blackie Blake again reassured the outlaws:

'That's dandy with me,' he managed a

parody of a smile, *'partners.'*

He had not, he hoped, dealt himself a hand that had loser written all over it.

CHAPTER FOURTEEN

Dan Clancy's head was full of the sound of thunder as the shock waves from the bullet which had grazed him, cutting a bloody furrow in his hair, reverberated. He lay perfectly still. He had little choice, the way his eyes were dancing all over the place. Slowly, he opened an eye to monitor the open stretch to the cabin. Should he try and make it to the cabin? Would the wobble in his legs be the match of the spinning in his head?

He heard Lucy's sobbing. It perked him up no end to think that she missed him. It was cruel to let her go on thinking that he was dead, but chances were that if he tried to enlighten her he would be dead, and fast.

The shots he had heard, he reckoned, had come from Bantry O'Shea. It pleased him,

161

too, to think that the Irishman, whose main task other than making moonshine was keeping his hide intact, had acted in his defence. He truly had not counted on the moonshiner getting involved. His practice had always been to stay out of trouble that did not concern him.

'O'Shea,' Lance Roebuck hollered. 'You hearing me, moonshiner?'

'Say what you've gotta say, Roebuck,' the Irishman replied.

'I've no quarrel with you. Clancy is dead. We can stop this foolishness right here and now. Are you willing to call it quits?'

'Are you willing to forget that I downed two of your men, Roebuck?'

'Let's say that they were stupid to get in the way of your bullets,' Lance Roebuck said.

'OK. Let's say that,' the moonshiner agreed.

Sorry that Dan Clancy had been killed, but pleased that he was not about to follow him into eternity, the Irishman stood up. The sniper Roebuck's chatter had gained time for to get into position, cut loose. Bantry O'Shea grabbed his chest and swore.

'Damn! You're one dumb bastard, Bantry. Should have expected nothing better than bottom of the deck dealing.'

The moonshiner pitched from the ridge. The crack of breaking bones as he crashed into the rocks below the ridge churned Dan Clancy's stomach. Lucy Bracken's agonized scream shattered the stillness.

'He killed two of my men, defending a killer,' Lance Roebuck said, in defence of his treacherous act. 'I couldn't risk him killing any more. The law will see it my way.'

'Sure it will, Roebuck,' Hank Bracken said, comforting Lucy. 'A bigshot rancher and a moonshiner. But in God's eyes you committed cold-blooded murder. And your judgement will come one day.'

'You understand, don't you, Lucy?' Lance Roebuck asked.

'I don't want you ever to come near me again, Lance Roebuck,' she said tearfully. 'For your evil deeds today you should be shunned by all decent folk. And I'll do my damnedest to see that you are.'

Hank Bracken said: 'We'll take Dan Clancy and Bantry O'Shea's bodies back to town for decent and Christian burial.'

Riled by Lucy's rebuke, the rancher railed: 'Do what you damn well like, Bracken! Mount up,' he ordered his crew.

Lucy and her pa were lifting Dan Clancy from the ground when he winked. Lucy, startled, dropped him back on the ground.

'Easy, Lucy,' he grinned. 'Don't want broken bones along with a pounding skull.'

No less startled, Hank Bracken said: 'Never saw a man play possum with such skill before, Dan.'

'Best let me be until Roebuck and his cut-throats have made tracks,' he told Lucy as she went to throw her arms around him, so great was her delight.

Lucy watched the Roebuck posse ride out of view, and then gave free-rein to her feelings, hugging Dan with the intensity of a bear.

'I love you, Dan Clancy,' she declared.

'About time you told me, ain't it,' Clancy said.

'Well now that you know, what are you going to do about it?' Lucy demanded to know.

Dan took her in his arms and kissed her until her toes curled, breaking away only when he saw Hank Bracken's critical gaze. Lucy, also becoming aware of her pa's look, which was close to outright disapproval, blushed as red as a summer rose.

'It's OK, Pa,' she said. 'I'm going to be Dan's wife.' Then, her certainty slipping when Clancy shifted uneasily, she enquired: 'Isn't that so, Dan?'

'Though I love you, I won't marry you, Lucy,' Clancy said. Lucy stepped back from Dan, the happiness of only a moment before vanishing like a puff of smoke from a bottle. 'I'm a drunk, Lucy,' he stated, harshly self-critical. 'No good to myself or anyone else.'

'Doesn't my loving you make a difference, Dan?' Lucy asked quietly. 'You can quit liquor. I'll help you.'

'Maybe I can break its hold, Lucy,' Dan said. 'And if I can, I'll be on your doorstep as eager as a new born puppy. That's the best I can offer right now. There'll be a lot better offers that you might want to take up in the meantime, and I won't blame you if you do.'

'But–'

'And I've got a charge of murder hanging over me,' Dan interjected.

Hank Bracken put his arm round Lucy's shoulders.

'Best leave it at that, Lucy,' he said. 'A man's got to face and conquer his own demons, before he's any good to anyone else.'

Lucy was not for leaving it be, but Dan Clancy's steely resolve left her with no option.

'I'll wait, Dan,' Lucy promised. 'There never was any other man. Or never will be for me.'

'I guess we'd best be headed back to town

with Bantry's body,' Bracken said.

'I'll bury him here,' Dan said. 'I figure that that's the way Bantry would want it.' He smiled. 'Never had no time for crowds and fancy trimmings.'

Clancy set aside Lucy's plea to remain with him.

'This is no place for a woman,' he said, entertaining no argument. 'Your place is at home with your folks, or back in town in your own shop, Lucy.'

'But Dan I want to be with you,' Lucy pleaded.

'Give me one week,' Clancy said. 'And if you don't see me clean and sober by then, forget you ever met me.'

'Come on, girl,' Hank Bracken urged Lucy, forcing her into the saddle against her will. 'Dan is being fairer than any man I know.'

Lucy Bracken rode away, the trail swimming in her tears.

The emergency meeting in the back room of

the general store in Watts Bend was like all hastily convened gatherings made necessary by the threat of danger, frenetic.

'Sam Brody was right,' Willie Sneed the livery owner grumbled. 'He said that if we didn't rein in Lance Roebuck, we'd get vermin like the Bellews on our doorstep. Now who the hell is going to face up to Frank and Ike Bellew? That's what I'd like to know.'

Ned Drucker, the Town Council chairman, said: 'Lance Roebuck will talk sense to Frank and Ike Bellew. You'll see.'

'How d'ya figure that, Drucker?' The question came from the gangly Ed Rawlins, the town odd jobber. 'Seein' that it was Roebuck who invited the Bellews here to begin with.'

'Ed is right,' another man said. 'They'll be looking to skin Roebuck alive for Junior Bellew's death, I reckon. If Roebuck's got a smidgen of sense, he'll put as much distance between Watts Bend and him as he can, and then some more.'

Drucker said: 'Lance is—'

'Trouble,' Rawlins declared. 'He's been trouble ever since Lucy Bracken fell for Dan Clancy. Losin' Lucy, loosed a devil in Roebuck.'

'I was talking to Art Spencer, the owner of the Big S only last week,' the town carpenter said. 'Told me that Roebuck wants to gobble up the entire range in these parts. I figure that the Bellews were hired by Roebuck as enforcers.'

'I figure that that might have been Roebuck's plan all right,' Doc Albright opined. 'The problem is, that with Junior Bellew dead, Frank and Ike will be wanting revenge.' The doctor drew on his clay pipe and let the smoke trickle down his nostrils. 'I think that the real danger is that the outlaws will take their revenge on Lance Roebuck first for failing to protect Junior. And then, with no law in this town, decide to make the town theirs.'

The businessmen at the meeting saw goods without payment flying out of their respective stores, and fretted. But the man with the biggest worry of all was Charles P. Taylor, the town banker. He quickly passed on his burden of worry to most of the gathering. The anxiety of those having accounts in the bank reached new heights. Most stood to have the goods from their stores purloined along with their bank accounts. Wiping out years of honest, and not-so-honest gains.

'We've got to appoint a marshal,' Taylor urged.

'Who'd be crazy enough to pin on a badge with Frank and Ike Bellew in this neck o' the woods?' Rawlins speculated.

Ned Drucker whined: 'Don't you think I've tried to find someone to take the marshal's job? Even offered double pay while the Bellews remain in town.' He shook his head. 'Don't reckon the town coffers have enough money to tempt any man.'

'Can't take it with you,' Willie Sneed snorted. 'And that's what a fella would want to be able to do, to be loco enough to face up to Frank and Ike Bellew.'

'So what can we do?'

Each man turned to Charles P. Taylor, his question ringing with desperation.

No one had the answer.

Dan Clancy watched Hank and Lucy Bracken until they were out of sight, fighting the urge to hare after them to be with Lucy. When they were lost from view on the twisting trail, Dan turned to burying Bantry O'Shea. Prayer had long ago been abandoned and forgotten when God had taken Sarah Browne from him, and had then seemed deaf to his pleas for help in dealing with his loss. But maybe He had a plan too. His words over the Irishman were simple ones. Then, task completed, he headed back to the cabin. He had a plan. How good the scheme might turn out to be could not be decided until its success or failure had been determined. He would face temptation and overcome it. Hopefully.

On reaching the cabin he prised up the loose floorboards near the fireplace, where he knew Bantry always kept a bottle stashed. He placed the bottle of moonshine in the centre of the table. Then he sat and looked at it, keeping his gaze steady on it, feeling his thirst sharpen. Sweat flooded through his pores until his body was drenched. The room spun. The bottle seemed to rise up and come towards him, trickling moonshine in front of him. In the tormented throes of his hallucination, Dan fought the urge to grab the bottle before the last drop was wasted. He fell off his chair and lay curled up on the floor, every nerve in his body twanging. His thirst grew and grew and burned holes in his brain. His lungs flapped, struggling to take in oxygen. His heart thumped, filling his ears with its erratic thunder. He was dying. Of that he was certain. But he was determined to die a dry man.

Dan Clancy mercifully passed out.

When he came to it was near sunset. Night followed, full of crazy visions and demons. The bottle on the table danced and mocked him.

Finally, exhausted, he slipped into a troubled sleep.

Jack Stone's sleep was troubled also. He woke, wondering why he was dripping with the sweat of fear.

'Doc,' he called out.

Then he recalled the sawbones had gone to a town meeting.

'Doc's not here, Jack.'

The curtain was blowing and the window was open. It had not been open when Doc had left. He had kept the window shut, because he feared that his patient, in shock, would catch pneumonia.

Blackie Blake stepped out of the shadows.

'Shit, Blackie,' Stone yelped. 'You darn near gave me a heart attack, lurking like a damn ghost. Lance send you?'

'Yeah, you might say that.'

'What's going on in town, Blackie?'

'The Bellews rode in, Jack.' Stone went rigid.

'Lance has talked to them? Set things to

right. Ain't he?'

Blake shook his head. Jack Stone began to tremble.

'Too busy,' Blake said. 'Looking after his own skin.'

By now, Blackie Blake's swaggering approach had brought him to Stone's bedside.

'Blackie,' Stone pleaded. 'You get hold of Lance, pronto. The Bellews will kill me.'

'No they won't,' Blake reassured Stone. His sneer was pure evil. 'I will.'

Jack Stone got only a fleeting glance of the stiletto flashing in Blackie Blake's right hand, before he felt its excruciating pain in his Adam's apple. Blake twisted the knife in Stone's windpipe, driving it deeper until the blade poked out of the back of Jack Stone's neck to skewer him to the bed. Then, drawing out the blade, Blake sliced off Stone's right ear.

Sneering, he said: 'Frank and Ike send their regards, Jack.'

His first act of devilry assigned him by Frank and Ike Bellew concluded, Blackie

Blake left the infirmary by the same route as he had entered. Dropping quietly into the dark backlot at the rear of the infirmary, he made swift progress to the saloon where the outlaws were hanging out, awaiting his return.

'It'll be a test,' Frank Bellew had said, when he had handed Blake Stone's killing.

'You see, we've got to know what kind of grit you've got before we rope you into the outfit,' Ike Bellew had added.

'And we'll need proof that you did as Ike and me wanted,' Frank said. 'What do you figure that proof should be, Ike?' he'd asked his brother.

Ike Bellew cast his eyes about before answering. 'Bring us back Stone's right ear, Blake.'

At the time, Blake had paled. Killing Stone was one thing. Disfiguring his corpse was something else.

'Is that a problem, Blake?' Ike had pressed him.

Blackie Blake was about to draw the line

and call it quits. But the way Frank Bellew's hand drifted towards his gun, soon had him agreeing wholeheartedly with the outlaws. It was that or die where he stood, he reckoned. However, now that he had done as the Bellews had instructed, he wondered why he had had qualms in the first place. He'd killed before, of course. But had drawn the line at taking trophies. However, as he hurried along to the saloon to meet up with Frank and Ike Bellew, the thrill of disfiguring Jack Stone's corpse was bubbling inside him, strange and exciting.

'We need a fast gun, and soon,' Charles P. Taylor pronounced to the meeting in the back room of the general store.

'Tell us somethin' we don't know, Taylor,' Rawlins said, his tone showing no respect for the most prominent citizen in Watts Bend.

'Where do we find such a man at short notice?' Willie Sneed, the livery owner wailed.

'It's a real pity Dan Clancy isn't around.'

All eyes focused on Doc Albright.

'Of what possible help could the town drunk be?' Taylor asked derisively.

'Saw him draw once,' the sawbones said. 'Lightning fast.'

'If he was, he sure as hell wouldn't be now!' was Taylor's brusque retort. A view that was heartily endorsed.

'Maybe handing Clancy the marshal's badge might just be the cure he needs.' The speculation was Albright's.

'You been sniffin' your own potions, Doc?' a man at the rear of the gathering called out. His levity brought a short-lived humorous break to the dour proceedings.

'In my opinion,' the medico said, 'all it would take for Clancy to overcome his liquor-fever, would be for someone to show a little confidence in him, gents.'

The doc's assessment had folk thinking for a moment before Charles P. Taylor dismissed the idea out of hand.

'There's no curing a drunk, Albright,' he

stated, in an uncompromising fashion. 'At least not a whiskey-chaser of Clancy's calibre, and besides, no one knows where he's gone.'

'Well, what the hell *do* we do then?' Albright barked. 'Let Frank and Ike Bellew take over our town?'

Blackie Blake slipped unnoticed into the saloon and joined Frank and Ike Bellew in its darkest corner. Proudly, he placed Jack Stone's severed ear on the table, the blood still fresh on it. Ike Bellew picked up the trophy and examined it, opining:

'Real pretty ear.'

'Am I in?' Blake asked.

'You're in,' Frank Bellew said.

'That means you buy the drinks, Blackie,' Ike said.

'Sure, *partners,*' Blake said, going eagerly to the bar.

Ike Bellew threw Jack Stone's ear into a nearby spittoon. 'Are you serious about him riding with us, brother?' he enquired of

Frank Bellew.

'No,' Frank answered. 'We'll kill him when this is all over.'

Ike Bellew looked to Blackie Blake, hurrying back from the bar with their drinks.

'Never saw a dead man move as fast,' he sneered.

Seated at the partially open window of the sitting-room above the dressmaker's shop, Lucy Bracken watched as men filed out of the general store, the town meeting having broken up. Smaller groups gathered in the street, still debating. The general opinion seemed to be that all the town could do was to hope and pray that the Bellews' revenge for Junior Bellew's killing would not be too drastic. Someone should tell them, Lucy thought, that hope and prayer where the Bellews were concerned, would be about as effective tools as wickless candles in the dark. Spitting guns were the only persuaders that Frank and Ike Bellew would understand. Doc Albright was hotly arguing his point of view with a group of men coming across the street, who finally ended up underneath Lucy's window.

'I tell you gents, that we should seek out Dan Clancy,' the town sawbones was saying. 'Therein lies this town's only hope of curbing the Bellews' revenge. Which I believe will be fiercesome.'

Lucy's ears perked up. And when the doc went on to repeat his assertion from the meeting that someone who cared was all that Dan needed to kick his liquor habit for good, her heart beat a little faster. But only momentarily. Her hopes for Dan's admittance to town society were dashed when, as before, the men with Albright threw cold water on the idea of Dan ever amounting to anything.

'Besides,' it was Ned Drucker the Town Council chairman who spoke. 'How could we have a killer as a marshal.'

Lucy was about to fling wide the partially open window and deliver a fiery defence of Dan when a rider going by, a man she recognized as a Roebuck cow-puncher, said: 'Or a ghost either.' All eyes were on the rider. 'Clancy's dead,' he declared. 'Lance Roebuck shot him.' He rode on. ''Night folks.'

Lucy had almost made a great blunder. Had she come to Dan's defence, promoting Doc Albright's point of view, she would have revealed that Dan was alive.

'You leaving town, Larry?' a man who knew the cow-puncher asked.

'Sure am, Andy,' the rider said. 'This town and the Roebuck range is about to have big trouble. I prefer to earn my dollars in a lead-free atmosphere.'

He rode on into the dark.

A drunken trio emerged from the saloon, supporting each other – Frank and Ike Bellew, and their new cohort Blackie Blake. They collided with a man who was making his way home from the town meeting.

'Steady on, fellas,' he said inoffensively.

'You saying we're drunk, mister?' Ike Bellew growled, eager to pick a fight with the hapless man. The man, knowing the degree of danger he had unluckily stumbled into, looked to the other men nearby, all of whom looked away. 'I think he called us low-down drunks,' Ike proclaimed to his brother and Blake. 'And that's real insulting, don't you boys think?' Without further ado, Ike Bellew drew and shot the man. He laughed. 'That'll teach the critter some manners.'

Everyone left on the street scattered under a hail of wild lead from the trio. Trouble had finally – as the late Sam Brody had predicted – come to Watts Bend.

CHAPTER FIFTEEN

A bloody week ensued.

Lance Roebuck's emissary, sent to talk with Frank and Ike Bellew, had been dragged behind a wagon until he was raw meat. Roebuck had taken to hiding out in line-shacks, moving continuously between several in the hope of evading the Bellews until their anger eased, and he could parley with them. Good sense told him that he should have rode out as fast as the wind, but he was loath to lose his grip on the ranch lest his uncle, relieved of having to look over his shoulder all the time, would slam the door shut on him. And he was too ambitious a man to let the prize of the Roebuck range slip from his grasp.

A continuous stream of Roebuck hands, liberally compensated for the risk they took in going to town, reported back the stubborn nature of Frank and Ike Bellew's anger.

'There must be some deal that can be done!' Lance Roebuck yelled at the latest hapless messenger from town.

The cowering cow-puncher said: 'Word is that the Bellews are going to stay put until you show up, Mr Roebuck. There's also word that another couple of hardcases are on their way to flush you out of these hills.'

Lance Roebuck snarled: 'Are the Bellew boys too scared to try and flush me out themselves?'

'They don't see no sense in riding into country they don't know, handing the advantage to you.'

Puzzled, Roebuck said: 'It doesn't make sense for them to lounge around in town. I could be long gone by now.'

The messenger's eyes slid away from Roebuck's. Pieces suddenly falling into place, Roebuck grabbed the cow-puncher's shirt front and yanked him on to his toes. He rifled his pockets with his free hand, coming up with a bundle of dollars from his trouser pockets – much more than he had paid him to scout town.

'Talk!' Roebuck growled, putting his sixgun to the man's head.

'I ain't the only one taking Bellew money, Mr Roebuck,' he whined. 'Mosta the fellas you send to town give as well as get inform-ation.'

Lance Roebuck's anger exploded with the ferocity of a volcano blowing its top. He pushed the man away and delivered his pistol's full chamber into him.

Lance Roebuck's anger abating, fear took over. He hurried to the door of the line-shack to scan the country outside. For the first time, he realized that money cannot buy friendship or trust. He felt alone, un-protected and totally vulnerable. A bird rising from a nearby thicket had him leaping back into the cabin, sweating. Perspiration flooded out of every pore. He wondered how long it would be before someone would think of delivering him up to the Bellews.

He quickly gathered up his belongings and sought out another line-shack. Watching, Frank Dawson wondered how much the outlaws would pay for Lance Roebuck on a platter?

Lucy Bracken had waited longer than she could bear. A week had passed, if only marginally. Maybe Dan was sick? Making up her mind, she made her way to the livery, which like every other business in town had been more or less taken over by the outlaws and their willing agent Blackie Blake.

'Could I please hire a horse, Willie,' she enquired of the livery owner, conscious of Blake lounging against the livery gate. 'I want to ride out to see my folks.'

'Howdy, Miss Bracken,' Blake greeted Lucy leerily, his eyes roaming over her form with undisguised lust. 'I'd sure like if you'd invite me to call on you sometime soon. I'd like us to be friends.'

'I'd rather kiss a rattler, Blake,' Lucy flung back.

Blackie Blake's eyes narrowed. 'That a fact.' He strolled towards her, his mood ugly. 'And what if I want to call on you an'way?'

'I'll kill you if you try!' Lucy stated boldly.

Blake laughed, and gave an exaggerated shiver. 'Now you've got me all scared, Lucy, honey.'

'Leave her be,' Willie Sneed said.

'An'one talking to you?' Blake snarled.

Sneed handed Lucy the reins.

'Tell your ma and pa I send my best regards, Lucy.' Lucy mounted up. Blake blocked her way. 'I said leave her be, Blake,' the livery owner repeated.

Luckily for Sneed, the angry impasse was broken by the sound of gunfire. Blake hurried to the livery gate to monitor the street. Charles P. Taylor was staggering from the bank, holding his gut, blood pouring freely from a terrible wound.

Blake laughed. 'I guess Taylor finally got the guts to object to Frank and Ike Bellew helping themselves to the bank's cash.'

187

Silent, stunted people, crowded the board-walks in a sombre vigil over the banker's body lying in the dusty street. Frank and Ike Bellew came from the bank, waving fistfuls of dollar bills. Blackie Blake hurried to join them, a full partner in Frank and Ike Bellew's celebrations.

'Best if you use the back exit, Lucy,' Willie Sneed advised Lucy Bracken. 'And when you reach home, you stay put 'til this trouble's over.'

Though tempted to parade her defiance by riding along Main Street, Lucy did as the livery owner suggested. But she did not tell him – could not tell him – where she was bound. She hoped as she rode out of town, that she could remember the trail to the late Bantry O'Shea's cabin. And she prayed that when she got there, she would find Dan Clancy alive and well.

If she did not, her life would be over then and there.

CHAPTER SIXTEEN

For a whole week Dan Clancy had kept the bottle of moonshine as the centrepiece in the cabin, until finally he could look at the bottle and not quake all over. His torment had passed. But he was wise enough to know that for the rest of his natural life there would be a demon dogging his tail, always ready to spring should he ever waver in his determination to never again taste liquor. He felt good and took pride in what he had achieved. He could now look at the bottle of moonshine; look at its sparkle and imagine its taste, and not get a thirst that heated his brain to melting point.

He wallowed in the fresh water of the creek a short distance from the cabin, eventually washing away the grime of years, which had collected on his skin and clogged his pores.

'Judas!' he exclaimed, his nostrils now clear enough to pick up his own stench. 'You must have had folk running every which way when you put in an appearance, Clancy.'

He dived his head beneath the water and pulled back up showing his face to the sun, feeling and appreciating its radiant warmth on his skin for the first in a long time. His thoughts turned to Lucy Bracken. He had been a fool. And he had been the luckiest critter in the West that Lucy's love for him had endured even his shameful slide into disgrace. For a woman to stand by the kind of half-hog/half-man he had become, took a whole lot of courage and a mountain of love. Which made Lucy Bracken a woman in a million.

So deep were his thoughts of his future with Lucy, that he did not hear the breaking of a twig until it was much too late, should his visitor be any threat. He spun round in the water, conscious of the gunbelt he had left on a boulder at the edge of the creek. He had long ago traded his own gunbelt for a bottle of rye, and the gunbelt he now possessed had belonged to Bantry O'Shea. Maybe, he thought, it would not make a whole lot of difference had he had the gun strapped on. He had once been fast, but there was nothing like liquor to slow a man's responses.

The second the rider appeared out of the trees on the slope of the creek, Dan's eyes glowed with the warmth of a Christmas fire.

'Lucy!' he yelled, and was standing upright in the water before he realized it.

'Dan Clancy!' she exclaimed, averting her gaze.

Dan, suddenly aware of the picture he had presented to Lucy, sank back under the water. 'Sorry, Lucy. I was just plumb over the moon to see you.'

'Are you decent now?' Lucy asked.

'Sure I am. But I can't stay soaking all day long.'

When Lucy turned her gaze back to him, Dan Clancy's heart did a jig on seeing her sheer pleasure. 'I was worried out of my mind about you,' she scolded him playfully.

'While all the time you were lolling about and frollicking in this creek.'

Behind her jocular joshing, Lucy knew how hard a time Dan had gone through. His agony was there in the deep lines of his face and his burned-out eyes. He had got a whole lot thinner. But that could be corrected with a dozen or so healthy meals.

'I'll mosey off into the trees,' she said. 'While you make yourself decent.'

'You won't peek,' he ribbed.

'And what if I do?' Lucy said brazenly. 'I'll only be seeing now what I intend to see a whole lot of in the future.'

'If your pa heard you, gal,' Dan chuckled, 'he'd shoot me and horsewhip you.'

As Lucy rode off to the cover of the trees, Dan waded out of the creek and dressed quickly.

'You can come out now,' Dan called out.

Lucy came forward all right, but in the hold of a critter as ugly as a mule's behind, accompanied by another specimen of man whom God would be hard pushed to categorize as human. Dan dived for the holstered sixgun on the nearby boulder. There was a time when he would have easily claimed the weapon and be shooting in the seconds which had passed. But now his muscles were leathery and unyielding, and his hands awkward. He fumbled and dropped the sixgun.

A bullet whined off the boulder. Mule-face levelled his pistol on Clancy.

'Next bullet will be right through your ticker, mister!' he promised.

Clancy stood perfectly still. Mule-face's partner came down to the creek. He filled his greasy hat with water and put it back on his head full, letting the water rush over his face and upper body.

'Hot, ain't it?' he said, in the kind of friendly tone one decent-minded traveller might use to another. 'Name's Mike Donovan.'

Dan Clancy's spine tautened. He had heard the name before. Donovan was a cutthroat who sometimes rode with the Bellews. His reputation was such, that he could slit his own mother's throat and lose no sleep. Dan's glance went to the man holding Lucy prisoner. Ed Barley, he reckoned, Donovan's constant saddle companion, a honcho whose reputation was tenfold more fiercesome than Donovan's. Barley liked women a lot, but not like other men did. It was said that the pleasure he took from a woman was not a normal man's enjoyment: story had it that Ed Barley's pleasure came from the pain he inflicted on a woman, rather than from the pleasure to be enjoyed from a good-looking woman.

Mike Donovan had a reputation as a tracker second to none.

'I like your girl, mister,' Barley told Clancy. His hand cupped Lucy's breast and squeezed until her face filled with pain, but she refused to cry out. 'Really like her,' he sneered.

'Touch her once more and I'll kill you, Barley!' Dan swore, knowing how futile his threat was under the circumstances.

'What're you goin' to shoot good old Ed

with, mister,' Donovan mocked. 'Your twinkle?'

As Donovan bent double laughing, Clancy carefully measured the distance between them. Confident in his superiority, the wily outlaw had come closer to Dan than would be the norm. Barley, too, was relaxed, and enjoying his partner's crude humour. Obviously both men saw no threat in the weedy specimen that Dan Clancy had become. Their mistake. Clancy's advantage. He had only seconds to act.

Lance Roebuck's departure from the line-shack he had been hiding out in was monitored by Frank Dawson, using the cover of the wooded slopes to track him. Dawson had not yet decided on his course of action. He could stick with Roebuck in the hope that the rancher would survive Frank and Ike Bellew's vengeance, and enjoy top dog status in the Roebuck scheme of things which, before the present upheaval, he had coveted. His second option was to sell out Roebuck to the outlaws for what he was certain would be a handsome reward – the Bellews having free access to the Watts Bend bank. Both choices had their rewards and their dangers. But which option was more likely to prevail when the dust settled. Knowing Lance Roebuck's new hidy-hole, Dawson turned back to the ranch, a man deep in thought, conscious of time fast running out.

'Sure is a dilemma, Frank,' he complained.

Riding to town with Lance Roebuck in tow, should he decide on that course of action, was not a prospect which Dawson relished. The nearer he got to town, the more desperate Roebuck would become. And the more desperate a man got, the more prepared to risk all he became. He could, of course, play safe. Get the drop on Roebuck and kill him. But there was no doubting that Frank and Ike Bellew would much prefer Roebuck alive and kicking. Delivering Roebuck dead might just anger them, with terrible consequences for the hapless messenger.

Word had it that the killer duo of Ed Barley and Mike Donovan had been summoned by the outlaws to flush out Roebuck. With Donovan's legendary tracking skills in play, it would take no time at all to run Roebuck to ground. Lance Roebuck could duck and dodge all he liked, but it would not matter a damn. Which meant that he had to act fast, should he opt for Lance Roebuck's delivery to the Bellews.

Dan Clancy sprang at Mike Donovan, hoping that surprise would outweigh what had to be the quicker reactions of the much fitter killer. As Clancy expected, Donovan's reaction was lightning quick. He spun, the .45 on his right hip clear of leather, but not yet cocked. There were only feet between them. But was the short distance too much to leap before Donovan's gun exploded? The thought of what would be Lucy's fate at the hands of these bastards, sent adrenalin surging through Dan Clancy, giving him the impetus he needed. As they crashed to the stony edge of the creek, Clancy cleverly swung the off-balance outlaw to form a cushion to protect himself against the searing damage that the jagged stones would inflict.

Donovan's scream on colliding with the rock-strewn ground filled every inch of space in the creek and surrounding hills. His body jerked violently and his back arched, dislodging Clancy, whose hold on the outlaw was tenuous. Donovan was clutching at his back, his mouth still opened wide but soundless. Dan Clancy's stomach heaved on seeing the dagger sharp segment of rock protruding from Mike Donovan's back, blood pulsing from a wound that had laid bare his spine. The serrated rock, its teeth sharper than any knife blade, had severed the outlaw's spinal column. Mike Donovan shuddered and fell back into the creek, welcoming death.

The curve of the creek's slope had unsighted Ed Barley, and he had not seen the final outcome of Clancy's lunge at his partner. But the bloodcurdling scream had stood his hair on end.

'Mike!' Barley hailed. 'You OK?'

Clancy forced himself to shake off the horror of Mike Donovan's death. He looked around frantically for the outlaw's pistol.

'Mike!'

Barley's shout was nearer.

Finding the gun, Clancy quickly made his way to the blind side of the slope and climbed it to get behind Ed Barley. He saw Barley, Lucy still his prisoner, peer cautiously over the edge of the slope into the creek. On seeing no sign of Clancy, and Donovan's body bobbing in the creek, Barley knew instantly where Clancy had got to. He was about to pivot around when Dan ordered:

'Stay right where you are, Barley! Let the girl go.'

'And if I don't?' Barley snarled.

'I'll shoot you where you stand,' came Clancy's steely reply.

'In the back?'

'If that's what it takes,' Dan promised.

'Chances are that with me holding your

girl as tight as I am, the bullet would pass through me and into her. Do you want to take that risk?'

'No, I surely don't,' Dan Clancy said. 'But I will, rather than let Lucy suffer the vileness you'll visit on her.'

'I think you're bluffing, mister,' the outlaw stated confidently.

'Do you want to take that gamble, Barley?' Dan said tersely.

'Maybe,' the killer said with casual ease. But the stiffening of his shoulders told Dan Clancy another tale. He was rattled. Therefore, like all wild animals, highly dangerous. Clancy figured that a compromise might resolve the stand-off that, if continued, would grow more deadly by the second.

'Just let my woman go, Barley. That will end our quarrel. Then you're free to mount up and ride out of here in one piece. The other choice is to remain right here with a bullet hole in you.'

Though Lucy Bracken was finding breath scarce with fear, her joy at Dan Clancy's description of her as *my woman*, was undeniable.

'You killed my partner, mister. Don't you reckon that you should have to pay for that?'

'No. Mike Donovan was less than human and deserved killing,' Dan stated bluntly.

The outlaw laughed.

'Yeah, he was a pretty mean bastard at that. And I figure that he's not worth dying for.'

'Then we have a deal?'

Barley's shoulders hunched.

'But then again, this fine woman might be worth the risk of dying for,' he said.

'My patience is running out fast,' Clancy growled. 'Dally any longer and I might just shoot you for the hell of it anyway.'

Dan glanced at the gun he held, and wondered. The gun had been dropped at the muddy edge of the creek, and his tumble into the creek with Donavan would have set up ripples which might have washed over the pistol. In which case, if the water had seeped into the gun's chamber, it might be useless. And he would not know either way until, and if, Ed Barley chose to gamble.

With the ranch in sight, Frank Dawson drew rein and turned his horse. His decision reached, he made quick time back along the trail to the latest line-shack that Lance Roebuck was holed up in. He had decided that Roebuck was more than likely finished, and therefore he had better declare for Frank and Ike Bellew, pronto.

'Hey, friend,' Ed Barley said. 'I accept your terms. You can have your woman.'

Released from captivity, Lucy ran towards Clancy. Too late, Dan saw Ed Barley's plan. He had anticipated Lucy's eagerness to reach Dan by the most direct route, and in her joy had come between the killer and Dan, cutting off a clear shot from Clancy without risking Lucy's life. Barley, grinning wolfishly, spun round.

He held all the aces.

CHAPTER SEVENTEEN

Dan dived for Lucy, taking her in a rough-house tumble down the slope. Barley's bullets bit the ground around them. Clancy and Lucy were fortunate to avoid serious injury, and reached the end of the slope none the worse for wear, except for some bruises and scratches. Clancy shoved Lucy into a clump of undergrowth. Lying flat out, he made himself as small a target as possible. Ed Barley's latest load ripped a chunk of bark from a nearby tree. A sizeable segment of it clouted Dan on the side of the head, for a moment sending him reeling. Recovering quickly, he pulled the trigger of the .45 just as Barley loped down the slope for the kill. The gun gave a hollow clank. He pulled the trigger again, with the same disheartening result. The creek water had done its worst.

All he was holding was a chunk of useless metal.

Lance Roebuck restlessly paced the shack, incessantly checking the terrain outside. He saw no sign of another presence. So why had he a sense of being watched? At first he had put his unease down to raw nerves. But so persistent was the feeling, that it became obsessional. When a mouse skittered across the floor of the shack, he almost leaped out of his skin.

Roebuck wiped sweat from his face. He inhaled deeply to settle down his thundering heart. But there was no stopping its thumping, erratic beat.

Ed Barley's cackle made Dan Clancy's blood run cold.

'Looks like Mike was right, mister,' he goaded Dan. 'You're going to have to shoot me with your twinkle.'

In desperation, Clancy pulled the pistol's

trigger for the third time. Only a fizzle of sparks left the gun's barrel.

'Looks like I'm going to get the woman after all,' Barley sniggered, drawing a bead on Dan Clancy. 'When you reach hell, tell Mike Donovan I said hello.'

In a last throw of the dice, Clancy again pulled the trigger of the .45. *Pssshooo!* Dan was a surprised man when the gun blasted. But he was not the most surprised man around. That *hombre* was Ed Barley, already on his way to join Mike Donovan.

Lucy, ragged with tension clung to Dan. He held her gently, his nostrils full of her scent. For the first time in a long time, there was something more important to him than a bottle of rotgut.

Lance Roebuck relaxed as he saw Frank Dawson ride up. If there was one man in the entire Roebuck outfit he could trust it was Dawson. He hurried to the shack door to open it and greet his visitor. But, hand on the latch, he paused. How did Dawson know where he was?

Roebuck backed away from the door.

'Lance? You in there?'

Roebuck relaxed again. Obviously, by the nature of his question, Frank Dawson was looking for him on spec. 'Yeah,' he immediately responded. 'Come right in, Frank.'

Letting out a sigh of relief, Dawson dismounted and strolled casually to the shack. He had almost made a fatal mistake, had he not realized in the nick of time that simply walking right up to the shack would have indicated knowledge of Roebuck's residency. By asking if Roebuck was at home, he had stymied any thoughts along those lines by Roebuck.

Frank Dawson could already feel the bulge of Bellew dollars in his pocket.

Mounted up, Dan Clancy led the way down the hill trail from Bantry O'Shea's cabin, conscious of the good friend he was leaving behind.

'Are you sure that going back to town is

the right thing to do, Dan?' Lucy worried. 'We could just ride clear of this territory.'

'I don't have a choice, Lucy,' Dan Clancy said sombrely. 'You know that. I'm not going to start our life together with me as a wanted man.'

'I don't want to lose you, now that I've just found you, Dan,' Lucy said.

Clancy squeezed her hand in his. 'You won't.' He wished that he could be as positive in his mind as he sounded in his words.

Building storm clouds quickly darkened the sky. Dan looked to their milling darkness, and saw in their aggravated swirl, the match of his own emotions.

His doubt eliminated, Lance Roebuck heartily greeted Frank Dawson: 'Good to see you, Frank.'

'Is that fresh coffee I smell?' Dawson asked airily.

'Just brewed,' Roebuck confirmed.

'You wouldn't mind pouring a cup for a thirsty visitor would you, Lance?' Dawson asked genially.

'My pleasure, friend.'

Lance Roebuck turned to the pot-bellied stove to fetch the coffee pot. For a second he could not understand how the afternoon had got so suddenly dark. Not until the pain inside his skull exploded from Dawson's gun butt. Roebuck plunged into blackness, cursing his stupidity for trusting any man when there was a reward to be collected.

CHAPTER EIGHTEEN

About three miles from Watts Bend, the storm broke. Dan Clancy welcomed the cover it would provide him with. Storms kept folk indoors. He hunkered down in the saddle and pulled the brim of his hat low over his eyes.

'I want to be with you, Dan,' Lucy had complained, when he had dropped her off at her folks' house. But he would not bargain with her.

'The town is in the grip of lawlessness, Lucy,' he told her. 'And you're too important to me to have anything happen to you.'

Dan was not sure what benefit his trip to town would bring him. In hope, he was looking for some clue that would free him from the shadow of the gallows. He had no doubt in his mind that Lance Roebuck had

had a part in Sam Brody's murder, if he was not actually the marshal's killer. But proving it was the big problem – his big problem.

As he rode on, Clancy constantly exercised his gun hand, desperate to get the feel of his pistol and regain the speed with which he could once draw. Of course there was no chance at all in the short time available, for him to reach any where near his old proficiency. That would take weeks if not months of practice. All he could hope for was, should he have to, that he would be able to draw and not fumble. His hands had got steadier, but no way steady enough. His reflexes, too, had improved. All he had to do was find that vital clue, or get that all-important break. And, of course, to survive the next couple of hours.

Lance Roebuck's plight was acute. Watts Bend was getting closer by the second, and his fear of what awaited him heightened. Mixed in with his emotion of fear, was one of throbbing anger at himself for being duped. Though his wrists were raw from his struggle to free himself from the rope binding his hands behind his back, Roebuck still maintained the futile exercise, hoping beyond hope.

'No point,' Dawson told him for what must have been the hundredth time, on observing Roebuck's struggle. 'Even if you managed to free yourself, I'd kill you.'

'I doubt that,' Roebuck said. 'Deliver me dead, and you'll be joining me soon after, I reckon. But...'

Frank Dawson turned in his saddle to look at Lance Roebuck.

'You sound like a man with a proposition, Lance,' he said.

'OK. Forget this crazy notion of handing me over to Frank and Ike Bellew,' Roebuck cajoled. While promising himself that should Dawson accept his offer, he'd kill him the first chance he got. 'I'll make you top dog at the ranch with pay to match.'

'That the best you can do?' Dawson sang out, unimpressed.

Roebuck sweetened his offer.

'A full partnership when old Nathan kicks the bucket.'

Dawson shrugged. A little more impressed, but not won over.

His desperation peaking, Lance Roebuck pleaded: 'I'll make you a very rich man. Rich enough to settle where you want.' Dawson drew rein. Roebuck grinned. 'Interesting, ain't it?'

'Rich?' Dawson probed.

'Rich,' Roebuck confirmed.

Dawson, to Lance Roebuck's amazement rode on, delivering a thunderbolt.

'Gotta say no, my friend. You see, you're a rattler in a sack, Roebuck. And once you get out of that sack, you'll still be a rattler with all the instincts of a rattler.' He looked hard-eyed at Lance Roebuck. 'You'd kill me first chance you got. And then, of course,' he reasoned, 'Frank and Ike Bellew might kill you before you handed over all that cash, and that would leave me with a pile of nothing. So I reckon that I'll take my chances with the Bellew boys.'

'I'll kill you, Dawson,' Roebuck raged.

Untroubled, Frank Dawson rode on, hauling Lance Roebuck to his grisly fate.

As Dawson approached Watts Bend from the east, Dan Clancy was riding in from the west. On the outskirts of town, he diverted to the late marshal's residence, in the hope that some vital clue that would nail Sam Brody's killer would be found there.

Clancy stabled his horse in a shed out back of Brody's house, not wanting the mare to be spotted by a curious passer-by. It was unlikely that there would be anyone about in the storm, but he had learned the hard lesson that fate often showed a mean streak when least expected. He entered the house through the kitchen window and stood in the eerie silence, made even more pronounced by the fury of the storm. The storm had turned the day to premature night, filling the house with shadows. Dan had a sense of being watched by Sam Brody's ghost.

'If you're around, Sam,' Clancy said with a weary sigh. 'Let me know what happened here. Because there's a noose waiting to stretch my neck for your murder.'

Dan started as the parlour door creaked. A second later he was laughing at his foolishness. The breeze blowing along the hall was the ghost. He made his way upstairs to the late marshal's bedroom, the scene of his untimely death. There was the sound of distant gunfire. The Bellews acting up, he reckoned.

On the eruption of gunfire, Blackie Blake looked down from the church tower where he was acting as a look-out. A man staggered out of the saloon, gut shot. Ike Bellew followed him outside and shot him in the back.

'Pure waste of lead,' was Blake's opinion. 'He was already a dead man.'

'Anyone got any objections?' Ike Bellew drunkenly hollered above the storm. There was no answer. The streets had long been deserted, and not solely because of the storm. He cut loose with a hellish yell and peppered the air with lead.

Frank Bellew, a saloon whore on each arm, put in an appearance.

'Ike, you're giving me a headache,' he groused. He pulled one of the whores to him and kissed her hard, while he shamelessly fondled the other woman. 'I'm in a loving mood, Brother.' He diverted his attention to enquire of Blake: 'Anything moving out there, Blackie?'

'Naw, Frank,' came back Blake's bored reply. Then, seeing movement, he peered into the gloom and quickly changed his mind. 'Riders! Two!'

'That'll be Ed Barley and Mike Donovan, I reckon,' Frank Bellew declared delightedly.

'Don't think so, Frank,' was Blackie Blake's opinion. 'One of 'em's hog-tied.'

Disappointingly, Sam Brody's bedroom yielded up no clues as to his murderer. In dime novels there would be a shred of cloth that could be matched to the killer's uniquely patterned silk vest. Or the impression of a boot print which had a star-shaped flaw in the heel. But that was in dime novels. Dan searched the remaining rooms, and came up empty. Despondent, he went back downstairs and left as he had entered via the kitchen window. Without evidence, how would he ever prove his innocence of Sam Brody's murder?

Blackie Blake's excited holler about riders coming was carried on the storm to Clancy's ears. Door hopping, he made his way along Main Street to Lucy's dressmaker shop which, again, he entered through a back window. He quickly made his way upstairs where he slid open a window to eavesdrop on the happenings in the street.

Frank and Ike Bellew were standing in a downpour outside the saloon, awaiting the arrival of the riders. As they drew near, Dan recognized the lead rider as Frank Dawson, a Roebuck hardcase. It knocked him for six when the identity of the second man, Dawson's prisoner, became known – Lance Roebuck. Drawing rein, Dawson told the waiting outlaws:

'I figure that my load is worth a pretty penny to you gents.'

The Bellews did not disagree.

'Why don't you step down to parley, friend,' Ike Bellew invited Dawson.

Dawson, believing he had gained acceptance, welcomed the outlaw's invitation. He had one foot on the ground when Ike Bellew sank his knife into his back. Frank Dawson fell, jerking legs churning the mud. Ike Bellew slit open his belly.

Lance Roebuck, his terror reaching new heights, began laughing like a wild hyena as his sanity was stretched to breaking point. Babbling, he tried to forge a deal with Frank and Ike Bellew, unsuccessfully so.

'I'm going to skin you inch by inch,' Frank Bellew promised the blabbering Roebuck.

Lance Roebuck screamed out: 'Someone, help me!'

All doors remained steadfastly shut. All ears as deaf as stone. Dan Clancy never dreamed that he could have pity in his heart for Lance Roebuck, but found that he could not remain immune to his awful suffering. He slid open the window and stepped on to the roof of the overhang.

'Cut him loose!' he ordered Frank and Ike Bellew.

Ike Bellew was the first to feel the burn of Clancy's lead in his gut. Blackie Blake, who had come running to join in the terrorization of his former employer, was second. Cornered, Frank Bellew bargained.

'The town bank is busting at the seams, mister. Take all you want.'

'I don't want a solitary nickel,' Dan answered stonily.

'Kill him, Dan,' Lance Robuck screamed.

Doors along Main were now opening. Men were coming from the saloon. All amazed at who was calling the shots and saving the town.

'Don't you have something to tell these

good folk about Sam Brody's murder, Roebuck?' Dan demanded.

'Sure I do.' Roebuck called out at the top of his lungs. 'Dan Clancy did not murder the marshal. Jack Stone did.'

'It's easy to blame a dead man,' Ned Drucker said.

It was as Drucker said, easy to blame a dead man for what Clancy was convinced was Lance Roebuck's crime. Dan did not care either way. The shadow of the gallows was gone from him. The mood of the citizens was such, that Lance Roebuck was washed up in Watts Bend anyway.

'Shoot Bellew,' Roebuck again demanded of Dan Clancy.

Clancy holstered his gun.

'My business in this town is finished,' he said.

'Well mine ain't!' Frank Bellew snarled.

In a flash of a second, Frank Bellew was lifted clear off his feet and blown halfway across the street. Bellew was fast, but Clancy had been faster. And if he wanted, with a little more practice, he'd be faster still. But he had other priorities. He threw the sixgun into the mud, dropped down from the overhang of Lucy Bracken's shop and walked away.

Dan and Lucy talked long into the night, and decided that their future lay elsewhere.

'California, maybe,' was Dan's speculation.

'Wherever you want to go, Dan,' Lucy said, love gleaming in her green eyes. 'I'll be there with you.'

Martha Bracken was grief-stricken when they told her of their decision. But Hank Bracken saw the sense of a new start.

'New man, new beginnings,' was his wisdom.

Ned Drucker led the Town Council members in a plea with Dan to become the new town-tamer of Watts Bend. But Dan told them plainly that his interest in the town and its citizens was nil.

Seated on board the wagon which Hank Bracken had generously gifted them, Dan

Clancy asked his new bride:

'Are you sure about this, Lucy?'

'I've never been more certain of anything in my life, Dan,' she said.

Exhilarated, Dan Clancy said: 'Then let's make tracks, Mrs Clancy.'

The crack of the whip over the team hauling the wagon, had a merry ring that no whip had a right to have.

The publishers hope that this book has given you enjoyable reading. Large Print Books are especially designed to be as easy to see and hold as possible. If you wish a complete list of our books please ask at your local library or write directly to:

Dales Large Print Books
Magna House, Long Preston,
Skipton, North Yorkshire.
BD23 4ND

This Large Print Book, for people
who cannot read normal print,
is published under the auspices of
THE ULVERSCROFT FOUNDATION